*Once Ghosted,
Twice Shy*

Also by Alyssa Cole

Reluctant Royals
A Princess in Theory
A Duke by Default

Coming Soon
A Prince on Paper

The Loyal League
An Extraordinary Union
A Hope Divided

Off the Grid
Radio Silence
Signal Boost
Mixed Signals

Other Works
That Could Be Enough
Let Us Dream
Let It Shine
Be Not Afraid
Agnes Moor's Wild Knight
Eagle's Heart

Once Ghosted, Twice Shy

A Reluctant Royals Novella

ALYSSA COLE

AVONIMPULSE
An Imprint of HarperCollinsPublishers

Excerpt from *A Prince on Paper* copyright © 2019 by Alyssa Cole.

ONCE GHOSTED, TWICE SHY. Copyright © 2019 by Alyssa Cole. All rights reserved. Printed in the United States of America. No part of this book may be used or reproduced in any manner whatsoever without written permission except in the case of brief quotations embodied in critical articles and reviews. For information, address HarperCollins Publishers, 195 Broadway, New York, NY 10007.

Digital Edition JANUARY 2019 ISBN: 978-0-06-293186-3
Print Edition ISBN: 978-0-06-293187-0

Cover design by Nadine Badalaty
Cover photographs © Kevin Kozicki/Getty Images (couple); © Sergey_T/ iStock/Getty Images (background); © axis213/Shutterstock (legs)

Avon Impulse and the Avon Impulse logo are registered trademarks of HarperCollins Publishers in the United States of America.

Avon and HarperCollins are registered trademarks of HarperCollins Publishers in the United States of America and other countries.

FIRST EDITION

19 20 21 22 23   HDC   10 9 8 7 6 5 4 3 2 1

Once Ghosted, Twice Shy

Chapter One

Winter

"ATTENTION, PASSENGERS, WE apologize for the delay."
The MTA conductor's voice was tinny, but the exaspera-
tion rang clear as the voice fuzzed through the speakers
in the stalled subway car. "We are being held momentarily by the train's dispatcher due to a malfunctioning
signal. Or something. Thank you for your patience. We
will be moving shortly. Maybe."

Likotsi Adelele, mother of schedules and slayer of
inefficiencies, would usually have been quite annoyed
with her train being stuck on a bridge for half an hour
with no explanation, but it was a special day: she had off
from work. The full weekend! Two days to herself, a re-
prieve from managing meetings with dignitaries, heads
of states, and business interests; planning royal dinners,
royal date nights, and royal relaxation; and overseeing
most aspects of the life of His Royal Highness, Bringer

of Light and Love, Prince Thabiso Moshoeshoe of The-solo, currently situated in Manhattan.

Or more time to think about her.

Likotsi tugged at the thigh of her trousers—teal gabardine with a matching blazer—before crossing her leg so that an ankle rested over her opposite knee, exposing bright yellow socks. She brushed away a speck of dirt that had lodged in one of the diamond-shaped perforations that decorated the aged tan leather of her new brogues. Her father had mailed her the shoes a few weeks back, a Christmas present to go under the giant fir tree lodged into a corner of the royal townhouse, since Naledi enjoyed partaking in Christian holidays. When Likotsi had finally been allowed to open the package, held hostage until four a.m. on December 25 by an ever vigilant Naledi, she'd discovered a note inside: *New shoes point toward the future, sweet daughter. You cannot keep wearing that which you have outgrown.*

Likotsi had slipped the note and the shoes into her closet for the two weeks following the holiday. Today she would break them in, walking away from memories that should've evaporated long ago but had left residual damage, like stains on suede after a sudden downpour.

She winced as the conductor made another announcement, this one completely unintelligible static.

A train delay was fine. A train delay was *delightful*. Anything she encountered this weekend would be delightful because she was tired of the dejection that had nagged at her for months. Dejection was inefficient, and worse, it was pedestrian. Moping and wallowing had left a green tinge on the memories of her few perfect days in New York the previous spring, like the band of a fake gold ring. It was time to leave the shoes she had outgrown behind.

It was time to create new memories.

As far as interminable train delays went, being stuck on the Manhattan Bridge on a Saturday morning was about as good as one could get. Outside the window of the train, the January sunlight was dappling over the choppy, ice-strewn waves of the East River, tinting the muddy waters a silvery green-gold. The cold blue of the morning sky seemed endless as it stretched out over Brooklyn on one side and Manhattan on the other, holding all the promise of the recently arrived New Year.

A week before, Likotsi had watched the ball drop from the apartment of a translator she'd met at the UN. As she'd walked home, surrounded by drunken revelers, she'd wondered what it would've been like to kiss Fab at midnight instead.

No thoughts of her today. Enough.

On the Manhattan side of the river, the sharp angles of the skyscrapers were burnished with light, making it seem as if the impossibly tall buildings were sunbathing. New York City didn't have majestic mountains or roaring waterfalls or rolling plains, like her homeland, but it was a beautiful city in its own way. It deserved better than to be the receptacle of memories that impeded her forward motion like a badly tailored suit that was too tight at the knees and elbows.

Likotsi had been working double duty as assistant to both Prince Thabiso and Naledi, his betrothed, for months. She'd been particularly dedicated to her job for the last seven months and three weeks, happy to work long hours and not just for the supplemental pay. Thabiso had gone from gently asking that she work less to outright commanding it.

She supposed she had been very . . . focused on keeping their schedules and making sure everything ran like clockwork.

The goat that wanders is the goat that gets lost. She hadn't allowed herself to be lost to the pain of stinging rejection, especially over such a fleeting affair. She had *focused*, stayed on the path of international relocation and American apartment hunting and making sure that everything in her boss's life was handled before he could think of it. There was a certain comfort in putting someone else's life to order when her own felt uncharacteristically messy.

But now she was on vacation. The last time she'd taken time for herself in this manner had been, coincidentally, eight months before, when Thabiso had been busy hiding his royal identity while wooing Naledi. Likotsi had downloaded a dating app and made the error of swiping right on Fabiola C, located 0.3 miles away.

Fab.

Fab's bio had been seven words: *Math. Jewelry. Dressing down is giving in.* Dark brown skin, Bettie Page bangs, and an hourglass figure were what had initially caught Likotsi's attention. Personality, talent, and drive were what had held it fast. An immediate, theretofore unknown connection was what had made Likotsi sure Fab was *the one.* Fab's blunt, cold breakup had shattered that illusion, but the shards remained.

Fabiola C: I can't do this. You're leaving, right? It was fun—let's stop before it's not.

Likotsi had thought the hurt would fade, eventually. It had been a temporary fling after all, and she was no slouch at those. While Thabiso had formerly held the title of the Playboy Pan Afrique, Likotsi had fared just as well in her own dating sphere, minus the fuckboy tendencies. In Thesolo, there were families anxious to settle their daughters with the prince's right hand, and when she traveled? Well, women found it hard to resist a sharp suit and a soft smile. Surely a woman she'd only spent a few nights with shouldn't have done her heart more than a glancing blow.

If Likotsi's obsession with efficiency had taught her anything, it was that sometimes it was the briefest setback that toppled everything afterward like dominoes.

On their second date, Likotsi had already been, as the youths say, ready to risk it all.

"What would this superimportant boss of yours do if you just . . . stayed?"

"I'm not sure. I've never thought of leaving. Until now."

Likotsi had considered that particular future while curled up in bed with the woman who had thoroughly captivated her. She loved her job. Thabiso was her friend, as well as her boss, but Likotsi had spent so much time planning his future that she'd severely neglected her own.

Two days later, Fab had broken Likotsi's heart, saving her the trouble of ever having to make a choice.

Likotsi had been living in Manhattan for five months now, having had to relocate along with Thabiso so Naledi could continue her education and they could continue their courtship, but she hadn't ever reached back out to Fab, whose last words had seemed final.

Likotsi: I thought you wanted more. Can't we discuss this?

Fabiola C: Sorry. No.

It'd been seven months and three weeks, and the woman's memory remained lodged in Likotsi's heart like a cactus thorn. She remembered the way Fab's smile always seemed a little bit wicked because the right side of her mouth raised up slightly higher than the left. She could still outline the shape of Fab's soft curves with her palms, if she closed her eyes. She could still feel the caress of deft fingers that created living, sinuous beauty from lifeless metal and raised goose bumps as they trailed over Likotsi's bare flesh.

Likotsi tapped at the sole of her shoe, a reminder. *Forward.*

Her phone vibrated in the inner pocket of her tan mid-length cashmere trench coat, which was slightly too thin for the weather but perfectly matched her shoes. Likotsi grabbed it and glanced at the screen.

AIRDROP—"MyNameIsAccurate" would like to send you a photo, the pop-up dialogue box on her phone read.

Likotsi looked around her train car. There were two teenagers sharing one set of earbuds between them having a subdued dance party, a couple holding hands and chatting intimately, an annoyed group of tourists taking angry selfies on the other end of the car.

A cute woman of East Asian descent seated diagonally to Likotsi glanced at her, then down at her phone, then back at Likotsi. Was she "MyNameIsAccurate"?

Likotsi's thumb hovered over her phone's screen. She was certain her phone was secure and that she wouldn't get a virus that might put His Highness's safety at risk, but she hadn't done any infosec training since before Christmas . . .

You're not working. And aren't you ready to finally start dating?

Likotsi accepted the photo.

Red leather gloves holding a section of drugstore receipt, onto which someone had scrawled, *Likotsi?*

She glanced over at the woman who had smiled at her, zeroing in on the woman's hands. Her gloves were of the dollar store magic variety, made of black polyester not red leather.

Her phone pinged again as a photo of a new scrap of receipt came through. *Are you back in New York?*

Likotsi sat still. There were few people who had known about her last trip to the city. Fewer with delicately tapered fingers who would wear bright red leather gloves.

The train lurched forward, finally resuming motion, and the tourists at the other end of the train car cheered, but Likotsi gripped her phone, staring.

This time the dialogue box offered a video, and Likotsi accepted with a mix of dread and, frustratingly, hope.

It was a short clip, starting with a tight shot of Likotsi through two smeared and scratched sets of subway train windows, her posture stiff and the shaved side of head exposed because she'd absentmindedly pushed her locs to one side while examining the photo she'd received. As the camera zoomed out, it became clear that the phone was recording in selfie mode. Out the shot pulled, revealing the stretch of smooth dark skin over high, sharp cheekbones. Out, revealing red-painted lips and familiar deep brown eyes.

The woman raised her pointer finger and brushed in front of the phone's camera—a swiping motion.

"Fabiola C, located, like, two feet away from you, has swiped right. Again," she said before flashing that wicked smile of hers.

Likotsi almost dropped the phone but managed to hold on to it—even a shock to the system such as this couldn't make her careless with her technology.

She stared at the paused image of Fab, with herself unfocused in the background, as if someone had managed to capture her state of being for the last seven months and three weeks. That was the version of herself she'd vowed to walk away from, and now the woman who'd caused her dejection had chosen today of all days to step out from her past.

She didn't tremble, and tears didn't prick at her eyes, but Likotsi felt slammed by the unfairness of it all. Her chest ached, and for a moment she hated everything that had brought Fab into her life the first time, and now the second.

She sucked in a breath against her own sacrilege— *Ingoka makes no mistakes* was a central tenet of her religion, the very root of everything Likotsi believed in. Still, she wished the goddess could exercise a bit more caution with Likotsi's feelings than had been taken of late.

The door separating one car from the other opened just as the train barreled into the darkness of the subway tunnel. The roar of the wheels on the tracks filled the car, and Likotsi's head whipped toward the noise. The train rocked back and forth as it sped toward Canal Street, but Fabiola C strolled in like a sailor used to rough seas, unbothered.

She looked . . . different. During the time they'd

spent together, she'd been dressed in meticulous pinup-girl style, but now that the initial shock was fading, Fab was beginning to come into focus.

Instead of a bright bandana or carefully set pin curls, Fab wore a blue knit hat with the white symbol of one of the sporting teams people in New York fought over. Her hair peeked out from under the cap, the tight curls framing her face by nature and not design. Her coat was of the knee-length down variety, black, and she wore jeans tucked into tan ankle-high work boots. She was still beautiful, but she was dressed . . . practically. It jarred Likotsi.

"I mean . . . hi?" Fab grabbed the pole over Likotsi's seat and looked down. Her eyes were wide, displaying her emotions like a mega-screen at Forty-Second Street, and what they advertised was shock and, more surprisingly, uncertainty. Fab's mouth twitched, but then she pressed her lips together.

From this angle, Likotsi could see Fab's earrings nestled beneath her curls: finely spun metal shaped into three-dimensional teardrops. How appropriate.

"Fabiola." Likotsi leaned back in her seat insouciantly, though she'd spent most of her train ride perched on the edge of her seat to avoid dirtying her coat unnecessarily. She refused to crane her neck up, though, and she didn't trust her ability to stand just then.

"The one and only," Fab replied with a mock curtsy. The overwhelming familiarity of her voice drove the cactus thorn deeper into Likotsi's heart.

Goddess, Likotsi loved a woman with confidence. She loved this one in particular. But love didn't change the fact that *this* woman had hurt her—that she could do the same if given another chance.

"Out of all the train cars in all the world you had to walk into mine." Likotsi switched up which ankle was resting on which knee, the action forcing Fab to take a step back, then tilted her chin toward the doors separating the cars. "You're only supposed to use those in case of emergency."

"I'd say that seeing *you* a few feet away counts as an emergency." Fab slipped gracefully into the empty seat next to Likotsi, crossing her own legs so that the toe of her boot almost grazed the sole of Likotsi's brogue.

She wasn't dressed in her usual style, but she smelled the same—like rosewater and orange blossoms and vanilla—and Likotsi wanted to hug her tightly and inhale, to fill her lungs with that scent she'd imagined waking up to every day.

Fab just looked at her, her expression so earnest that Likotsi started to wonder whether they really *hadn't* spoken for months. If, perhaps, there had been some misunderstanding when Fab had ended things.

It wasn't supposed to be like this.

Likotsi had imagined what would happen if she ran into Fab, especially since Naledi had mentioned how often she randomly encountered people she knew in this city teeming with strangers. Likotsi had fabricated a million droll put-downs. She'd mentally practiced the iciest cut direct known to humankind, one that would make everyone in the vicinity wince for Fab's bruised ego.

She would be *angry*.

Instead, she was confused. Nothing felt different. Now that the initial shock had faded, Likotsi found that the chasm of months that separated them felt no larger than a crack in the sidewalk. She wanted so badly to smile, to ask Fab how her day was going or why she was wearing a horrid mass-produced hat and coat.

She'd thought that Fab had smashed their connection like a smartphone beneath a car tire, but all their data had been saved on a cloud drive somewhere, it seemed, and was happily downloading and ready to resume where they'd left off.

No. She couldn't do that to herself again. Her official title was Advisor Most High, and she knew what pithy aphorism she would impart upon anyone who came to her with this problem: bind the finger before it is cut.

"That was very cute," Likotsi said, forcing steel into her tone. "The video and the swiping again. If this was a dating app, I would have had to swipe right, too, for you to continue the conversation."

Fab winced, but Likotsi paid the motion no heed. She'd had her day all planned out—it was a new year and she was wearing her walking shoes and she was going to be *done* with this—and now Fab had barged in, stirring up the emotions that Likotsi sought to settle.

"What are you in town for?" Fab asked, ignoring

Likotsi's jab. "I didn't expect you to be in the 'exes I awkwardly run into' category."

"You didn't awkwardly run into me. You spammed my phone with unwanted photos and videos to get my attention," Likotsi corrected. "How did you even know which phone was mine?"

"I mean, DandyQueen is pretty obvious." Fab was looking at Likotsi with an intensity that didn't match her tone, and when she spoke again her voice was strained. "What are you doing here?"

The question held a timbre of sadness and regret, one Likotsi had heard from Fab before.

"Why do you have to leave so soon?"

The irrational desire to hug Fab shoved at Likotsi again, but she held fast. She reached for her determination to move on, donning it like a sleek cape that would protect her from the pull of nostalgia.

"My job temporarily relocated to Manhattan. I've been here since September." Likotsi's voice was cold as an ice flow in the river. "You would have known that if you hadn't ghosted me."

Likotsi hadn't understood the term when Ledi and Portia had first explained it to her in terms of the dating world. *Ghost* was a noun, not a verb, but she'd supposed it had a certain poetic ring to it—disappearing like a ghost. It made more sense now that she put it in the context of having Fab this close to her again. It wasn't just the disappearing, but the grief as real as any loss.

In Thesolo, people didn't fear ghosts; they welcomed visions of the ancestors, but the aftermath was called a "second death" because you were forced to grieve again after that brief reconnection.

Oh goddess. Likotsi's throat was rough. *Would she have to go through that pain again?*

"I didn't ghost you. I told you that I couldn't continue the relationship," Fab said, the fingers of one hand lifting and her brows drawing together. "You were the one having a fling while in a different country for business. You were leaving, and stuff came up that made it clear I didn't have time for more heartbreak, okay?"

The train rattled as it rushed through the tunnel, the jerking motions pushing Fab against Likotsi and then pulling her away.

"You never responded when I asked why!" Likotsi's voice was brittle with a sudden anger as she struggled to be heard over the rattle of the train. Seven months and three weeks! That was how long she'd nursed this sorrow, how long it had been since her desperate messages to Fab had gone unread, and now Fab sat there with her warm brown eyes and bright red lips, calmly explaining that she hadn't done anything wrong.

"That's not ghosting, that's—that's having boundaries," Fab said gently. "You like knowing things, but the only things that mattered were that you were leaving, I was staying, and I had a life outside of our little fairy-tale trysts. I didn't mean to hurt you."

The train jumped a little on the track and Fab slid toward Likotsi, her body warm.

"Excellent. I give you thanks for taking time to explain boundaries to me. You and your boundaries could have stayed in the other train car if you really cared to enforce them."

Likotsi turned her head away, focusing on the tunnel lights blipping by at regular intervals. At least now she could finally close this sad chapter in her dating life and move on.

"Hey." Fab's voice was soft. Uncertain. "Did you eat yet?"

Likotsi glanced back at Fab. Her smile was wicked, but her eyes were tired and her face was strained.

That's not your problem, Likotsi reminded herself. She tapped her toe on the ground, reminding herself that her shoes pointed toward the future not the past.

She sighed.

"I had coffee and a butter roll earlier," she replied. And even though she knew she shouldn't ask, she did. "Why?"

"Have you had a chance to try dim sum yet? There's a place near here that's really good." She gestured out to the train platform as they pulled into Canal Street.

"I'm not hungry," Likotsi said.

"You like tea," Fab pressed. "They have great tea. Unlimited refills."

Likotsi knew she should say no. She'd made a resolution. She had an itinerary. She was going to walk the city alone, make new memories to blot out the ones featuring Fabiola's big brown eyes and her warm mouth. She was going to leave behind the itchy anxiety that had come with staring at unread messages in the dating app day after day.

But . . .

Her role as repository of wisdom had apparently also taken the weekend off.

"Dim sum is on my list of things to do." Likotsi patted the inner pocket that held her handwritten list, and she felt her heart beating fast beneath her palm.

"Can I treat you? To an early lunch?" Fab reached out, but then drew her gloved hands back. "I know this is weird, but I thought I'd never see you again. Like, I've been mad busy and this is my first free weekend in forever and—boom!—now you're here and you've *been* here for months, and—" She took a deep breath. "I'm rambling. I won't get ahead of myself, but maybe we can start with tea. And some soup dumplings?"

She stood and started toward the door as the train began to slow.

Likotsi stared at Fab, weighing her anger against her yearning, and though hope was a thing with feathers there was nothing insubstantial about it.

If she stayed on the train, she might never find out what Fab had hidden behind those boundaries—what had made her push Likotsi away. If she stayed, her shoes might never point forward.

The doors were open now. The passengers who'd been stuck with Likotsi were shuffling out and those who had crowded the platform waiting were flooding in, churning Fab through the doors and into the station.

Just sit. Let the doors close. Move on with your life.

Then Fab looked back, and those of eyes of hers hid nothing. There was no cunning—just cautious expectation.

The scale crashed down in favor of the fluttering in Likotsi's chest that fanned her anger and her curiosity and her longing.

Likotsi jumped to her feet and pushed past the people entering the train, body stiff as she tried to prevent too much damage to her jacket and suit, making it through the sliding doors just before they shut and the train pulled off.

This was probably a terrible idea, but then again, Likotsi didn't believe in coincidences. She'd made a vow to let Fab go, and then Fab had appeared, as if the goddess herself had conjured her.

The very practical side of her saw this for what it could be, without the chest fluttering—a reconnaissance mission. She'd spent months creating a shrine to Fabiola in her mind and her heart, extolling all the woman's perfections and lamenting the loss of them. She'd taken a negligible number of interactions and turned them into some divine experience that she would never be able to re create with another.

She would follow Fab's lead. She would remember

that Fab was a woman like any other, and that what they had shared was nice enough, but certainly not worth any further lamentation. Who knew? Perhaps she would find Fab to be utterly dull—as dull as the commonplace winter hat she was currently wearing.

Everyone on the platform was moving except Fab, a dollop of frozen relief. She seemed shocked that Likotsi had actually joined her. Then the right corner of her mouth kicked up.

"Took you long enough," she said, finally.

Somewhere, the polite part of Likotsi's mind chided her for blocking the flow of pedestrian traffic, but she didn't start walking. She slowly adjusted the lapels of her coat and then the hem of each cuff.

"Well. I'm certainly worth the wait."

Chapter Two

The Previous Spring

FAB FUCKING HATED first dates, but this time, for the first time since installing the dating app on her phone, she was more excited than nervous to be meeting someone. Maybe it was because she didn't have to worry about what this date would lead to— the woman she was meeting, Likotsi, had made it clear that she'd only be in town for a few days. Unlike most people Fab met on the app, Likotsi had been adamant about not starting things off under false pretenses.

Likotsi: I don't mean to be forward or presumptuous, but I value honesty: I'm only in this wonderful city for a few days, and my work occupies much of my time. If you're looking for something long term, I cannot provide that, but I've been told that I make pleasant enough company over a drink.

Fabiola C: Wooow. I'm intrigued by this honesty you speak of. Are you free this afternoon?

Likotsi: When? I've just been given leave to take the night to myself.

Fabiola C: "Given leave"? What do you do?

Likotsi: I'm an assistant to someone who requires a very particular skill set.

Fabiola C: <eyes emoji> Oooo, mysterious. I like mysterious. There's a great happy hour at my friend's bar in this neighborhood. It has a nice outdoor area, too. I'll be there in five minutes.

Likotsi: Then I'll be there in ten. Send me the address.

Fab had been heading to Lakay Sa Lakay Restaurant and Lounge anyway, carrying back Charles's tax documents, when she'd received the notification from her dating app.

When she'd seen Likotsi's photo—a woman in a dapper suit with a bearing that made her think of royalty and a mouth that made her think of worship—a flash of desire had zipped through her body, surprising her. Fab was a bit of a celebrity in her little pinup girl/ jewelry artist corner of social media, in the world that existed outside of boring tax statutes and documents sent to the IRS. Her feed was full of people posting the most flattering photos of themselves possible, but she'd never felt this potent attraction when scrolling through her timeline.

And it was more than the physical jolt of attraction: hope had flashed in her, like sunlight catching on a precious stone. Probability had started a plus and minus column in her head and her heart—then she'd read the message. Fab was tired of flings, but she'd wondered what that instant attraction would translate to in real life, and curiosity had won out.

In a way, she was glad this would just be a blip on the radar. She had her next few months planned out— preparing to give notice at the small accounting firm she'd been at since graduating, though she'd still do tax prep on the side during the busy season for the clients she'd acquired over the years. Her online jewelry store was doing well, and orders had been exploding as word of mouth spread. By the time Christmas approached, she'd have used her savings to rent a prime space at a holiday market. She wanted to turn her side hustle into her main hustle, and that would require all her time and energy, especially because she made her products herself.

Drinks with no expectations of more was about all she could promise anyone right now, anyway.

Her phone vibrated and she glanced at the text message, expecting it to be from her late date, but finding a message from her mother instead.

Maman: Lise has her check-in in two days. She told me she had a nightmare that she was trapped in a cage.

Fab: I looked over all her paperwork and everything is in order. It's been fine every year and it will be fine this year, too.

Maman: *Si bondye vle.* <prayer hands emoji>

If God wills it.

Fab sighed and put the phone away, not telling her mother that she'd also awoken from unsettling dreams about Tati Lise, the woman who had brought Fab her first jewelry-making kit one long ago birthday, stocking it with beads she'd brought back from Haiti. It was Lise who'd taught Fab, well, everything.

It'll be fine.

Likotsi's ten minutes had come and gone, and Fab was starting to cop a bit of an attitude. She sipped her water and stared at the door that led from the bar to the small tropics-themed backyard space with annoyance. Charles poked his head out, his thick brows raising toward his bald head. Fab scowled at him.

He disappeared back inside.

If she got stood up, at least it wouldn't have been after special date prep. She was wearing what she'd worn to take some springtime photos in Fort Tryon Park before heading to the lounge: yellow and lime-green wax print dress, sky-high heels, her hair soft waves from the pin curls she'd set before bed the previous night. If this woman didn't show, Fab could go home and edit her photos or watch some of the jewelry-making tutorials in the online course she'd signed up for . . . but Fab really hoped she would arrive.

And then she did.

Likotsi's hair was shaved on the sides, the edge-up fresh, with her hair on top long and twisted into locs. She wore a brown suit that had clearly been tailored to both accentuate her curves and minimize them, a starched white shirt that would have made Fab's Clorox aficionado mom proud, and gleaming brown leather loafers.

Likotsi looked as put together in person as she had in her photos, but her smile was much more becoming. There was a certain . . . regard in the tilt of her mouth, a mix of courteousness and insinuation. Like she would ask politely before giving you the best head of your life.

Heat rushed to Fab's face and she looked down to hide the thirst blazing in her eyes.

Her gaze landed on Likotsi's hands, and the bouquet of flowers they held. An actual bouquet. Yellow roses, purple carnations, and pink chrysanthemums, from the bodega down the street judging from the plastic wrap around them. Some people might make fun of flowers from a dusty corner store, but Fab always kept fresh flowers on the coffee table in her studio.

She always had to buy them for herself.

The attraction that she'd felt when she received the dating app notification was nothing compared to the odd, tangible certainty Fab felt in Likotsi's presence. They'd barely spoken yet and Fab *knew*. Whatever the night held would be good, and she needed something good to distract her from the gnawing worry about Tati Lise.

"Took you long enough," Fab said before wrapping her lips around her straw. She knew what she was doing with her mouth—Likotsi executed a polite bow, but her gaze rested on Fab's lips even as she bent at the waist.

"I got a bit waylaid," Likotsi said in a lovely accent that was clearly African, but different from the ones Fab had heard growing up in Brooklyn. "But I'm certainly worth the wait."

She handed over the flowers, and dammit, no bodega bouquet looked this good without some post-purchase arrangement. The flowers weren't supposed to assuage Fab because Likotsi was late—they were *the reason* Likotsi was late.

There was a fleck of green on the nail of Likotsi's well-manicured index finger, and the sight of it took Fab's resolution to enjoy this fling for what it was and reformed it into a heart-shaped wreath of yellow, purple, and pink.

Fab looked up, knowing the smile on her face was goofy as hell. "I think you just might be. We'll see."

Likotsi pulled out the seat across the table, her gaze intent as she adjusted her suit and sat down in one fluid movement. "Tell me your life story, the four-minute version," she said without preamble.

Fab's smile tilted into a grimace of confusion. "What?"

Likotsi relaxed into her chair, back straight and eyes knowing as she leaned toward Fab.

"I recently read an article that said there were thirty-six questions you could ask a date that lead to falling in love. Most of them are boring, though, so I'll only be asking you four."

"Are you trying to fall in love with me?" Fab laughed. "Before we even order our drinks?"

"Come. Your profile implies that you enjoy math. Four is only one-ninth of thirty-six. That's only a little bit!" Likotsi lifted one shoulder in a move too smooth and refined to be called a shrug. "I'm trying to fall a little bit in love with you."

On any other date, Fab would have rolled her eyes, or maybe plastered on a fake smile as she snuck a peek at her phone to see how long it would be before she could leave. But now she felt a slightly unsettling jolt of fear, like when she momentarily lost her balance on her high heels but righted herself just before she fell.

She rested her fingertips on the edge of the table and leaned forward a bit.

"Okay. Challenge accepted. My family came here from Haiti before I was born. I'm an only child. I grew up in Brooklyn, but live in this neighborhood now. I love food and travel, though I indulge the former more than the latter. I'm an accountant, which is sometimes not as boring as most people think it is, but my real love is making jewelry. I used to do it just for fun and my family, then I took some night classes at FIT and started getting serious. Now I have a small business and I'm looking to expand it soon."

Fab felt a little strange calling her online store a small business, but that's what it was, and something about how Likotsi sat with such self-assurance made Fab surer of herself, too.

"Impressive. When did you start making jewelry?" She looked appreciatively at Fab's necklace, giving a nod that felt like approval Fab hadn't asked for but was still glad to have.

Fab tilted her head. "Is this one of the four questions? If so, that's an oddly specific questionnaire or this is kinda creepy."

Now it was Likotsi who laughed. "No. That was my own question. I'm going off script."

"What happens if you end up asking me thirty-six questions, though?"

Likotsi brushed a couple of stray locs behind an ear with one hand. "Let's find out."

Fab sipped her drink just to look away from Likotsi's

eyes. She felt a little dizzy and she was still only drinking seltzer.

"I started making jewelry when I was a kid. My aunt enjoyed it, and when she saw how much I loved the stuff she made, she started teaching me. Brought me my own kit and taught me to make simple necklaces, bead bracelets, earrings, stuff like that. After I graduated college, I took classes on my own." Fab took a sip of her water. She was growing more nervous as the date went on instead of less. *Butterflies in your stomach* kind of nervous. "What about you?"

Likotsi rubbed her palms together absentmindedly. Fab looked at her long fingers and her short, well-manicured nails, and her face went hot yet again, a new record for her since blushing wasn't her usual reaction to anything outside of scandalous video clips her friends sometimes sent her and she accidentally opened in public.

"I am from Thesolo. I grew up in the country's capital, but most of my family lived in a smaller village, so I had the best of both worlds. I love technology, and travel, and interesting things."

Fab had heard some things about the country, possibly as questions in the lounge quizzes Charles held every two weeks, but didn't know much. It felt rude to say that, though, so she nodded as if she was well-versed in all things Thesolo.

"And you said you were here for work?"

For the first time, Likotsi looked a bit reticent, but she recovered quickly. "I'm an assistant to an important man in my country who is here for meetings and some other, personal business. He is very nice, if a bit thick-headed."

Fab was curious about the vagueness of Likotsi's work description—sometimes vagueness meant lies, but sometimes it meant protecting someone. It wouldn't be cool for Likotsi's boss if she was going out with randos from dating apps and immediately putting all his business on the street. She didn't press.

Likotsi pivoted quickly. "Is there something you've dreamed of doing?"

"This feels like a job interview," Fab said, rolling her eyes. "If the next question is 'What are your greatest strengths?' they're taking perfect selfies and memorizing federal tax codes."

She expected another question, but Likotsi just looked at her, that same curious, intent gaze.

Fab wasn't unused to being stared at—the way she dressed guaranteed that she at the very least got a passing glance wherever she went. But Likotsi wasn't looking at the jewelry or the clothing or the makeup. She was looking into Fab's eyes, her own full of mischief.

"What?" Fab swiped gently at the corner of each eye, making sure there was no crud.

"I was just thinking, *Goddess, I'm going to regret that swipe.*"

Fab raised her brows and lifted her almost empty

glass of seltzer. "Wow. We haven't even ordered alcoholic beverages yet and you've already fallen a little bit in love with me and started regretting it?"

Fab tried to look cool and unfazed even though the way Likotsi was staring at her—like Fab was the most interesting woman in the world—had her at fazed level: SHOOK.

"Yes," Likotsi said firmly. "Because I have one night to learn everything about you, and that isn't enough time. Not nearly."

Fab was a woman used to people spitting game. Men telling her how fine she was, women telling her she was fashion goals. This wasn't game. Because she understood what Likotsi meant, felt it in the way her heart was beating fast and her dress was suddenly too tight around her chest.

What in the world?

This was fun. Fun with a time limit. No need to start thinking about shit like love at first swipe.

She grinned. "Don't worry. There'll be a lot more things to regret, if the night goes well."

Likotsi nodded. "I'm going to hold you to that."

Chapter Three

Winter

LIKOTSI ENJOYED THE curious cacophony of the large banquet hall housing the dim sum restaurant—round tables filled with people who had nothing in common except a deep desire to eat as many of the small plates being rolled around the room on metal carts as possible.

Fab waved down the servers with assuredness, pointing out dishes she was clearly well acquainted with, and then handing over her paper menu, a food passport of sorts, to be stamped.

Likotsi could see why Fab had brought her there. The food was delicious, the tea was abundant, and it was about as public a place as anyone could hope for. One couldn't exactly have a deep conversation about life—or about heartbreak—while rubbing elbows with strangers and waving down food like it was a competitive sport.

But one could make *polite* conversation. Fab maintained a steady raft of surface level talk that kept them safe from the emotional barracudas swarming beneath them.

"Here, put the soup dumpling on the spoon first. Poke it to let out the steam. Pour this sauce on it and oh! You like hot sauce, get that chili oil. What have you been doing for all these months?"

"You told me about the porridge in Thesolo. Try this, it's called congee. Do you still use the app? I deleted mine. Nevermind, don't tell me. I'll get us some dessert."

She wasn't sure if this layer of obfuscating noise was a conscious decision on Fab's part, and was even less sure why she was pleased instead of annoyed when an hour had passed, their bellies were full, and Likotsi still knew nothing about why Fab had abruptly ended their relationship.

If Likotsi had thought Fab would quickly ease her mind, and then she'd be able to carry on with her day, she'd been mistaken.

"How did you find this place?" Likotsi asked.

"My friend in high school used to bring a group of us here sometimes," she said. "I would bring them to the Haitian spot in Canarsie. Another friend introduced us to the Indian buffets in Jackson Heights, and another to the Central American food trucks in Red Hook. We called ourselves the FF Crew."

She said the last part with a snort and a shake of the head.

"The fast and the furious?" Likotsi ventured.

"The food and fashion crew," Fab said. "We met in our school's fashion club and we liked trying different foods. The name was pretty literal."

Likotsi looked at the delicate silver earrings hanging from Fab's ears and almost reached out to touch one. Almost.

"Is that a new design?" She pointed toward Fab's earring, keeping her hand a safe distance away.

Fab cupped a silver teardrop between her fingertips. "No, this is from last spring. I haven't made anything new in a couple of months. Busy with work."

One of the busboys, a tall handsome man with spiky hair, came and removed their empty teapot and cups, looking pointedly at the crowd gathered in the waiting area as he did so, and Fab grabbed their food passport and stood, not elaborating further.

"Did you like it?" she asked as Likotsi followed.

Likotsi kept getting disconcerted that she didn't have to crane her neck to look up into Fab's face—Fab wasn't wearing heels after all. She'd been Amazonian in Likotsi's memory; maybe the love Likotsi remembered feeling was similarly larger in hindsight than it had been in real life.

"The food was delicious," Likotsi said courteously. "I loved trying so many different things, and the chicken feet were surprisingly good."

"You passed the chicken feet test!" Fab nodded approvingly.

Likotsi raised her brow. "Chicken feet test?"

"Yup. How someone reacts when presented with a new food they've never tried before, excluding dietary restrictions, of course."

Likotsi remembered their first date, when Fab had ordered several appetizers, explaining the Haitian names for the food. She'd been particularly pleased when Likotsi's favorite had been a kind of meat pie filled with hot dog, boiled eggs, and spices. Perhaps that had been a chicken feet test, of sorts.

Fab pulled out cash to pay, they headed toward the escalators, and a few moments later they were on the bustling Chinatown sidewalk.

Now that they were outside, Likotsi didn't have the distraction of a new experience to drown out the question she should have been asking herself.

Why did you follow her? Really?

They'd eaten and talked, and nothing had changed.

"I guess that's that," Likotsi said to fill the silence between them. "Thanks for your assistance in crossing off an item on my to-do list."

"And feeding you," Fab added as she stepped up to the window of a bakery, examining the items as if it was possible to eat a bite more after all the food they'd shared. She was acting like this was all totally normal, and the fact that it did feel normal, like they could slip back into their old affair like a vintage waistcoat, made it clear what Likotsi needed to do.

She took one last look at Fab.

"If that's all, I'll be on my way."

She didn't go on her way. She stood there trying to figure out what she'd tried to achieve. A task undertaken without an objective was a waste of time. Her objective, apart from her reconnaissance mission, had been waiting for the moment when she realized she didn't feel anything for Fab after all.

No, that wasn't true—Likotsi hated dishonesty and she wouldn't lie to herself. Maybe part of her was searching for reasons not to care for Fab, but the most important part in this situation—her heart—was waiting for everything to suddenly be all right.

She sighed.

If a goat bites you once, why put your hand back in its mouth? That's what one of Likotsi's exes had asked years ago, stubborn pride in her voice as she'd packed her things. But now here Likotsi was, offering her hand out to Fabiola like a novice herder.

She should have stayed on the train. Goat bites smarted quite a bit.

"What's next on your list?" Fab shivered, then shoved her hands in her pockets, doing a little two-step. "It's brick out here."

"Brick?" Likotsi asked, looking at the buildings above the shops that lined the street.

Fab shivered out a laugh. "Cold. It means cold."

"Right. Well, I'm going to walk. Explore."

Fab tilted her head. "I thought you had a list."

"I do. But I'm trying to be spontaneous too."

Fab grinned. "So your plan is to spontaneously visit a bunch of preplanned places? That's very . . . you."

Likotsi was on the edge of a cliff of indignation that was crumbling away, being eroded by the tides of familiarity. It was so easy, remembering how things had been between them, how they'd stuck to each other like two fashionable nettles and then blown where the winds of love had taken them.

It was only a few days.

She hurt you in those few days.

"Goodbye," Likotsi said abruptly, trying to save her fingers from the proverbial goat's teeth.

Fab exhaled deeply. "That's it?"

"*It* was when you ended things without explanation. This was a brief, random encounter. Now we'll both continue on with our lives."

There. That was closure. She'd spoken the words to Fabiola, and now they would come to fruition. It was like casting a spell, yes? When she clicked her heels and turned on the soles of her still too-tight shoes, she would leave Fab rooted in her past. She'd be able to enjoy dates again instead of comparing them to her, to go days on end without ever thinking of Fab's laughter or the way the pad of Fab's index finger felt skimming lightly over Likotsi's bottom lip.

Fab took a step closer, hands still in her pockets as she leaned forward to examine Likotsi's face.

"What if . . ." Her gaze was guarded, but determined. "What if I walked with you for a while."

It wasn't a question. Likotsi remembered something Fab had said to her as they shared a coffee from the same mug and she'd talked about a difficult manager at her job. *Asking permission is giving someone the power to say no.*

"Why would you walk with me?" Likotsi was unable to move away as she should have. She'd fallen for this siren song before, and she'd drowned beneath love's tempestuous waves. "Why would I want you to?"

"Because you said you were looking for spontaneity. I can give you that." Her tongue darted across her lips, pink against the red because her lipstick hadn't budged despite the dozen different foods they'd eaten. "I want to give you that."

Likotsi didn't know what Fab was playing at. Her job had given her firsthand experience with watching all kinds of liars as they wheeled and dealed with Prince Thabiso or other heads of state, and then dissecting what had been nonsense and why they had spouted the nonsense, the better to advise her prince. She'd thought that maybe she'd been blinded by Fab before, and that was why she hadn't seen the finishing blow coming.

But no.

Likotsi trusted her judgment, and it told her that Fab was being sincere, and that she had been sincere the first time they dated—that's what had bothered her about the brush-off. Fab had been straightforward, until that last interaction, when she wasn't. Likotsi didn't know what to do with that information, though. She didn't know how someone could seem to care for her, but also be so blasé about having hurt her.

Fab lowered herself back down onto her heels, eyes wide and mouth an "o" as if a lightbulb had just gone off in her head. "Hey. Hey! Yessssss, come with me."

She grabbed Likotsi's hand and turned, tugging Likotsi along with her. An icy winter wind slammed into them, blowing the hair that hung out from below Fab's hat back over her shoulders. Fab tightened her grip and looked back, a beckoning smile on her face that shattered Likotsi's resolve to leave.

You may ask of the goddess, but you may not dictate her means. Likotsi had prayed to be rid of her feelings for Fab, and it seemed that the only way over was through.

She didn't smile back, but she didn't pull her hand away. She followed the woman who trotted ahead of her, her red-gloved hand beckoning like a spring rose that had confused the seasons and bloomed in winter, bright and beautiful and defiant.

Fab led Likotsi away from Mott Street, down streets running parallel to Canal to avoid sidewalks clogged with tourists searching for discount bags and five T-shirts for twenty dollars, which Likotsi shuddered to think of.

They passed seafood shops with tanks crowding the windows, a park pavilion where people practiced tai chi despite the cold, an incongruous whiskey tavern, restaurants and optometrists and bakeries squeezed in between tourist shops.

A few minutes later, having passed out of Chinatown and into a neighborhood with different stores—trendier shops filled with expensive clothing, which made it all the more confusing when Fab dragged Likotsi into an alleyway that Naledi would have described as "sketchy as hell."

"Um." Likotsi stopped and tugged back on Fab's hand. "Has this all been an elaborate plot to steal one of my organs? I should warn you that they're currently being used and I won't part with them lightly."

She looked around at the alley, which wasn't infested with rats and covered with decaying food matter, but wasn't inviting either. "I said I wanted spontaneity, not an indecorous ending to my life."

Fab laughed loudly, the sound bouncing off the brick walls around them, hopping up the steps of the fire escapes bolted to the alleyway's walls, as if traveling toward the slate-gray sky above to open up a space of light that would mirror the one that Likotsi felt in her chest.

"Bloodstains would be way too hard to get out of these boots," Fab said, gesturing toward her feet.

"How comforting." Likotsi glanced around.

"Look down there. You see that door?" Fab pointed at a large black-painted steel door covered with graffiti that was swung out into the alley. "We're going there. Just trust—" Fab caught herself and pressed her lips together briefly before starting to walk again. "I think you'll like it."

Likotsi sighed and followed Fab, despite her lingering wariness. When she peeked around the door it didn't lead into a dark, creepy organ-harvesting factory, as she'd imagined, but a small, clean white room, lined with shelves. There were brief descriptions on crisp white rectangles of paper for each item.

"It's a museum," Likotsi said, delighted wonder filling her.

"Yes! A freight elevator turned into a museum. Only a few people can fit inside at once. Exclusive, right?"

"This is wonderful," Likotsi said. She knew that many people would ask what the point of something like this was, would find it precious or pretentious, but Likotsi adored things that took time and care to produce results that weren't entirely necessary but added something special to the world.

Fab stepped in beside her, eyes bright with excitement. "My little cousin told me about it, but I haven't had time to check it out. Look at this! Oh my God!"

She raised a gloved hand to her mouth to cover her squeal.

Each row of the selves was a separately curated exhibit, and Fab was looking at a row entitled "Objects removed from anal cavities during emergency room visits."

"Oh dear." Likotsi leaned forward and then away. "A two-liter bottle? Really?"

Fab squealed again. "There's a can of Raid! Why? How?"

"Perhaps there was an issue with cockroaches?" Likotsi guessed. "They can survive anywhere you know."

They looked at each other and burst out laughing, their glee filling the small space. Likotsi's face was stretched wide with mirth, the tug of her smile almost unfamiliar. It had been so long since she'd felt joyful silliness well up in her like this.

"This row is a bit more to my tastes," Likotsi said once they had composed themselves. "'Single shoes mysteriously found on the MTA subway tracks.' There's even a Louboutin!"

"Where did the other shoes go? How do you lose *one* shoe on the train tracks?" Fab asked, her arm pushing into Likotsi's as she leaned in to admire the Louboutin. "I would have jumped onto the tracks for this, deadass."

"Deadass? I think you're mixing up your exhibits," Likotsi said.

Fab rolled her eyes indulgently. "For real," she translated.

They spent the next twenty minutes going over the items in each exhibit, navigating the small space of the refurbished elevator together until they realized people were waiting outside. They reluctantly stepped out.

"That was great," Likotsi said. "They fit so much into a small space. Efficient!"

"I didn't even know there was a name for that plastic

thing that held the bread bag closed," Fab said. "So it was educational, too."

Likotsi looked around them and the irreverent joy that had distracted her from her predicament began to fade. They were standing in an alleyway—the museum had been a temporary escape from reality—one in which Fab was a woman who'd had her fun with Likotsi and then discarded her when it was expedient. She would have jumped onto the tracks for a Louboutin, but hadn't even seen Likotsi as worthy of a follow-up text.

Well, that puts things into perspective.

Likotsi gripped the collar of her coat against the cold breeze that funneled down the alley, kicking up scraps of paper and other detritus. In front of her, Fab executed a little spin, as if imagining herself in the skirt she'd worn on their first date.

"I haven't had that much fun since . . ." She stopped spinning, her arms still out and her gaze locked on the sky. "Since the last time you were here."

Likotsi sucked her tongue against her chattering teeth. "I find that hard to imagine."

Fab's arms dropped to her sides. "I . . . have a lot going on. Unlike you, some of us don't have fancy jobs that involve stays at luxury hotels and traveling all over the world, rubbing elbows with the rich and famous."

Likotsi mentally pushed up her sleeves in frustration, a measure of how mad she was because she would never treat an item of clothing so cavalierly. "That's one very narrow way to view my work, one that disregards the fact that I'm nearly always on call and have to put the needs of others before my own."

Likotsi expected Fab to say something rude back—maybe this was it, the moment where they would have it out, where she'd find out how Fab could have just *ended* things—but Fab just heaved a sigh and shook her head. "You're right. I'm the one who's new to that club. Hold on a minute."

She reached for her coat's pocket, pulled out her phone, and turned slightly away from Likotsi.

"Hey! Hi. You're there? Good. It's colder in Boston? Well, yeah, no sh—crap." She scuffed at the ground with the sole of her boot, then rocked back on her heels. "Yes, I know you've heard the word *shit* before, smartass. Uh-huh. Uh-huh. Okay. Be good. *Yes*, I'm out of the house. Yes, for fun. Nunya business. Call me after the competition. Love you. Bye."

She turned back to Likotsi as she slipped the slim phone back into her pocket, her gaze almost defiant. "My cousin," she said.

Likotsi nodded. "All right. Well, thanks for—"

"I think we need to, like, chill for a few minutes," Fab cut in. She was squinting off into the distance, as if envisioning something, and Likotsi considered running off while she was preoccupied.

This was one of the things Likotsi had found so attractive. Fab had always been planning ahead, seeing what was on the horizon. Perhaps that was why her rejection had hurt so much. Fab had looked toward her own future and there had been no place for Likotsi in it.

"Chill?" Likotsi asked, instead of running.

"Yeah." Fab said the word as if standing in alleyways and staring into space was totally normal, and it was Likotsi who was the odd one.

Honestly, it was absurd. She could have been almost to Canal Street already if she'd just left the freight elevator museum and kept walking. Fab could have been firmly behind her and out of her life.

But that's not what you want, is it?

"What do you have going on that's been keeping you so busy?" Likotsi asked, belatedly processing Fab's words from before her call.

Fab's head dropped to the side as her gaze pivoted to Likotsi. "Do you want to chill or nah?"

Oh, this was an anti-interrogation technique. Likotsi played this game with nosy reporters and people seeking favors of the prince and herself all the time. Respond to their questions with questions of your own and see who was willing to keep it going.

"Don't you have someplace you need to be?" Likotsi matched her tone to the frosty air rushing through the alley.

"Don't you want to explore the city and see cool shit?" Fab held out her hand again, like this was just so *easy.* Like they could just fall back into the way things had been between them. And the worst part was, it *was* easy. Likotsi had to shove her hands into her own coat pockets to resist the pull of how good it felt to be with Fab again.

"Why do I need *you* to do that? I was managing perfectly fine on my own until you interrupted my morning."

Fab's hand dropped a bit, but didn't fall back down to her side.

"I know you don't need me. It's just . . ." She looked away from Likotsi, but the rapid flutter of her eyelashes made it clear what she was trying to hide. "We had such a good thing. And I thought that thing was over. I needed to believe it was over. Then I saw you through the window on the train . . ." Her hand slapped into her coat with a muffled brush over polyester as it dropped to her side. "It's selfish, but I thought we could do what we did last time. Just have fun and pretend it won't hurt later."

Fab worked her bottom lip with her teeth.

"Did it hurt for you?" Likotsi asked carefully, taking a step forward without even giving the motion thought. "Later?"

Fab nodded hard, annoyed, but Likotsi knew the annoyance wasn't aimed at her.

"Of course, it did," Fab said, then grudgingly added, "It never stopped."

Well.

Well.

"Maybe . . . maybe chilling wouldn't be such a terrible idea." Likotsi reached out her own hand, heedless of the proverbial goat's teeth that threatened to close over her fingers. "Or maybe, like last time, it's a terrible idea but we'll ignore that part for now."

Fab tried to laugh, but the sound came out rough, choked. She took Likotsi's hand, her warm fingers closing quick and tight, like she would never let Likotsi go again.

"Come on." Fab said, and they were off.

Chapter Four

The Previous Spring

HAPPY HOUR AT Lakay Se Lakay was long over, and the crowd had changed from after-work drinkers reveling in a perfect Spring evening to those who'd come for the weekly Afrobeats dance party.

Fab wasn't drunk—she'd had two rum cocktails over the course of the several hours she'd spent talking with Likotsi, and they'd shared plates of fried plantains, pate kòde, and boulettes—but she felt giddy and happy and warm from the inside out. So freaking warm, like she'd found a vintage coat made of the finest, thickest wool, and sized exactly right for her heart.

Maybe she *was* drunk, not on alcohol but on the heady tension that was building between her and Likotsi. It was like a game of Jenga, with each new topic possibly being the one that would topple over the amazing and improbable structure they were creating together. Fab kind of wanted it to be knocked over because things shouldn't be this good with someone she'd probably never see again.

Likotsi lived on another continent. Both of them had acknowledged that long distance relationships weren't what they wanted as they'd jokingly expressed regret over their mutual attraction. The Jenga tower *needed* to fall, but Fab had a feeling it wouldn't. That they could build it up to impossible heights if given the chance.

Chance requires proximity, so no catching feelings.

She fanned her gaze out over the crowd, automatically scanning for Likotsi, who had gone to the bathroom. It was only now, sitting alone, that she realized that she was all in. This couldn't be more than a fun date, but . . .

No buts. NO. CATCHING. FEELINGS.

Then Likotsi appeared in Fab's line of sight, moving through the crowd with a jaunty fluidity that would have bordered on overkill if it weren't smoothly reined in. Maybe it was because Likotsi's job apparently entailed working with people who could buy out all the bottles in the VIP section, from what Fab had garnered, but Likotsi carried herself like royalty.

She wasn't conceited or anything, though she had every reason to be—she just seemed like she knew her worth. And she knew how to make others feel worthy.

Fab's last few dates, with men and women both, had been sub-par. That didn't make her special—dates being awful were the normal state of things these days. Her bad dates had ranged from incompatibility to potential partners being straight-up jerks.

Fab was an outgoing person, but she'd held herself back after a few dudes in a row who had seemed to want her stylishness and smarts as trophies, but would have been happier if she had no personality.

But Likotsi seemed to like Fab—to like Fab's words, and jokes, and ideas, not just the package they were wrapped in, though she clearly appreciated that, too. And Likotsi, with her old-fashioned charm, her kindness, and her humor? Fab couldn't help but like her back.

Dammit.

Likotsi sat down across the small table, her smile loose. She'd taken off her suit jacket while she was in the bathroom—it was draped over the back of her chair now—so there was only the stark white of her French placket shirt against her smooth dark skin. The shirt was still tucked in, but the sleeves had been carefully rolled to mid forearm. Fab realized with a start that Likotsi's tie was gone, too, and the top two buttons of the shirt were undone, revealing the shadows between the slopes of her breasts.

"Ahem."

Fab glanced up to find Likotsi watching her with a knowing smile.

Busted.

Fab grimaced and fanned a hand in front of her eyes, then pulled it away. "Shit. Sorry! I didn't mean to . . ." *Eye fuck you.* ". . . creep on you."

"I wouldn't call it creeping," Likotsi said cheerfully. "Perusing."

"That sounds much more dignified," Fab said with a slow grin.

Likotsi laced her fingers together and rested her forearms on the edge of the table—she hadn't done that while she'd worn her jacket. Fab found it oddly attractive that Likotsi's rolled sleeves had a function other than "increased sexiness," though that was the result.

If Likotsi only changed her attire for functional reasons, why had she removed the tie and unbuttoned her shirt, revealing the fine hollow at the curve of her neck and the swell of her breasts?

"I believe that I'm going to have to call you out on something," Likotsi said.

Fab felt a tremor of unease. Maybe the Jenga tower was about to tumble down and, wow, that wasn't what she'd wanted after all.

"What?" she asked a little sharply.

"Earlier you said that if we were here late enough to dance that you would, quote 'put it on me.'" Likotsi stood again and walked around the table. "I'm not quite sure what that means but I think I'd like you to show me. Can I have this dance?"

Fab might have laughed at Likotsi's chivalrous manners, but there was *intent* in the woman's eyes, and there was nothing chivalrous about that. Likotsi wanted to touch her—they weren't about to get up and line dance after all. The couples already on the dance floor were pressed close against one another, hips winding to the bass-driven music.

Likotsi led her into the crowd inside the lounge, then turned . . . and stood there.

Fab leaned close to her ear. "What's wrong?"

"I actually can't dance very well," Likotsi said. "Even when I do the traditional dances back home, I'm always placed at the back of the group. You've been warned."

It wasn't a self-conscious confession. Even in admitting something that could get her made fun of, Likotsi met Fab's gaze and grinned. Fab felt the *liking* and the *wanting* that had been building up in her all evening smash into one another. She shouldn't have worried about catching feelings—she should have worried about losing her grip on them.

"Well, I wouldn't want you stepping on these shoes," she said in a low, calm voice, as if her heart wasn't beating wildly in her chest.

She slid her hands around Likotsi's waist, watching to make sure that she wasn't crossing any lines. Likotsi didn't pull away—she stepped closer to Fab until there was no space between them except the wrinkles of their clothes bunching as they pressed together.

"You can lead," Likotsi said, heat and mischievous light in her dark brown eyes. She rested her hands on Fab's shoulders and pushed her hips forward just slightly. The contact of their hip bones made Fab's stomach go fluttery with desire.

"Something tells me you aren't used to following," Fab said, easing into a swaying two-step that Likotsi followed after an initial misstep in the same direction.

Likotsi slid her hands behind Fab's neck, lacing her fingers so that her warm palms rested on Fab's nape. There was the slightest mismatch of tempo in their shared rhythm and Fab sped up to adjust, recalibrating the whine of her hips so that they were soon back in sync.

"You're right," Likotsi said with a grin. "But you don't have to lead to get someone to follow you."

They both laughed, and Fab's forehead brushed Likotsi's. "Why do I feel like I'm getting a side of life advice along with my sexy dancing?"

"It's my accent," Likotsi said, brows raised. "Americans seem to think I sound very wise. Also, I must correct you. This dancing is not very sexy because I don't really know how to move my hips. I can only move in one direction. See?"

Fab laughed a little, but mostly she focused on the way Likotsi was suddenly undulating against her with more emphasis, almost riding her leg. It made her think of the way Likotsi might move against her in the privacy of Fab's apartment, how, if she shifted her thigh and tugged down on Likotsi's waist, she could press her thigh up and—

Fab's nipples went taut beneath her bra, and desire throbbed between her legs.

"I think we might have different definitions of sexy," she said, though the way Likotsi's lips were slightly parted insinuated that Likotsi knew exactly what sexy was and that she was being pretty damn successful at it. "But here you go."

The music switched to a slower tempo and Fab slipped her thumbs through the belt loops on the back of Likotsi's pants, holding her in place as she began to work her own hips.

"Move like this." She swung her hips in a slow, loose figure-eight motion, grinding against Likotsi so she could feel the motion and also because Fab wanted her.

Sweat beaded on her upper lip, despite the fans pointing at the dance floor—her whole body was warm.

Likotsi had overstated her inability to dance—she caught the rhythm of the music, gaze still locked on Fab's, and her hips worked just goddamn fine.

"Like this?" Likotsi raised her brows, almost in challenge. Her head was tilted up, her mouth close to Fab's neck, her exhalation tickling along the sensitive skin there.

Fab nodded, bringing her mouth dangerously close to Likotsi's. "Just like that."

Fab enjoyed flashy dancing, had practiced all the latest dance crazes with her friends, but she didn't move away from Likotsi even when the music changed to a faster song. They moved their bodies against one another, the friction of their breasts brushing and the winding of their hips more than dancing now. Likotsi did keep losing the rhythm, but Fab didn't think it had anything to do with skill. At that point, she was barely paying attention to the music herself, focused only on the parts of her body touching Likotsi's body and how to keep that contact going.

Likotsi leaned up to Fab's ear after several songs had passed. "Can we step outside for a moment?"

"Sure." Fab was a little breathless herself.

Outside it was cool, the spring night air not yet taking on the steaming mugginess of summer in the city. Fab closed her eyes against the pleasant breeze, which carried away the heat on her skin but not the desire in her belly.

The street was mostly quiet, apart from the lounge—it was a weekday after all. Fab had work in the morning. She should be going home, doing her nightly skin-care routine, and getting some rest.

"Sorry to drag you away from the dance floor but"— Likotsi stepped closer to Fab—"the music was so loud, and when I ask 'Can I kiss you?' I want to hear your answer loud and clear."

"Yes," Fab breathed.

"I didn't ask yet," Likotsi said with that grin of hers.

Fab cupped Likotsi's face in her hands and leaned down until their lips pressed together.

Likotsi's lips were full and soft, and her mouth was warm as her tongue pressed back against Fab's. Fab leaned into the kiss, her mind clear of everything except for the taste and scent and feel of Likotsi. They swayed in the cool spring night, kissing and kissing until Fab wasn't even sure how she was still standing.

"I have a room at a luxury hotel in Midtown," Likotsi breathed against her lips.

"Oh, fancy," Fab chuckled. "But far. Too far. My studio is around the corner."

"I'll go grab our things," Likotsi said.

Fab leaned her head back, and then brought her chin down to her chest. "You know, I'd forgotten I even had a purse in there. It takes a lot to make me forget an accessory."

Likotsi plucked at her collar. "So I'm 'a lot.' Is that a good thing?"

"Yeah." Fab leaned down and kissed Likotsi again, not caring if someone was making off with her vintage purse in the meantime. "Real good. I can't wait to show you how good."

"Goddess," Likotsi breathed against Fab's mouth, the exhalation full of humor and anticipation and reverence. "You're gonna put it on me, aren't you?"

Fab laughed. "Just you wait."

She went back inside, and Fab pulled her phone from her skirt pocket.

Maman: Fabiola, do you have the number for the lawyer? Just in case? You know I hate this texting. Call.

She put the phone away and tried not to think about *just in case*. What that would mean for her family and, more selfishly, for her. Guilt nagged at her, that she was even thinking about herself.

Tomorrow, Likotsi would be gone and she'd call her mother. Tonight, Fab would have fun.

Chapter Five

Winter

THEY LEFT THE alley the way they came, and this time Fab wasn't pulling Likotsi, though she still had her by the hand. She walked a step ahead, as if worried that Likotsi would decide against going along with whatever it was they were doing if she moved into the lead position.

"Your cousin is on a school trip?" Likotsi asked. She fully expected to receive "Nunya business" as a response, but Fab answered without hesitation.

"She's up in Boston with her school's debate team for a competition." The words seemed clipped, hurried, as if she didn't want to talk about it. "It's this fancy private school—they do cool, but mad expensive, stuff like this all the time."

Likotsi doubted it was as fancy as the private school in the Alps that Prince Thabiso had attended, but perhaps it was as expensive given how much everything in New York seemed to cost.

Likotsi had a vague memory of Fab having stopped by her cousin's school before meeting for coffee on their third date. "How old is she again?"

"Seventeen now. A senior in high school." Fab stopped in front of what appeared to be a French bistro. "Here we are."

"I'm not sure I could eat again just yet," Likotsi said, though she did begin to look over the menu hanging in the window. A tiramisu might go nicely with a cup of coffee.

Fab gave her side-eye. "It's above the restaurant. Come on."

Likotsi looked up at what appeared to be a normal four-story apartment building—a solid rectangular brick, like the others on the street.

When she glanced at Fab, her expression was pensive.

Maybe she's ready to talk, Likotsi thought, and though she had wanted to know why Fab had broken off their relationship—though that was the reason she was even following her, wasn't it?—she felt a tremor of unease at finally knowing.

They went into the entry and up two flights of stairs, tracing the smoky scent of incense up to a door with the word *DREAM* stenciled on it. The smell reminded her of stepping into the priestess's temple, but with heavier, more pungent aromas than the delicate natural odor of eng oil.

The apartment had a look somewhere between ascetic and "went wild at Drukanese wholesale store." The walls were a stark white, free of any hangings, and the floors were clean, dark wood, but the floors were scattered with pillows in rich purple, blue, and pink, edged with gold. Low wooden coffee tables of wood with the Drukanese bodhisattvas carved into them appeared every few meters, with incense burning in receptacles at their center. Dark, heavy curtains blocked the winter sun so that the play of a light show—first green, then blue, and then purple, undulating through the room like ripples on water—were visible. A kind of atonal music played in the background, Zen but modern.

"Hmm. This is where we're going to chill?" Likotsi looked around. A white man with a beard sat crosslegged in one corner, hands resting on his knees and eyes closed. "I thought it was going to be an ice cream parlor or something."

Fab scoffed. "Like I'd be busting out Mr. Freeze-level puns. I'm not *that* corny."

"Well. An ice cream shop has a purpose. Whereas this place . . ." Likotsi shrugged, ignoring the way Fab narrowed her eyes. "I can sit and stream weird music at home."

"Or you can sit with me. I'm giving you *culture* here." Fab took her hand again, leading Likotsi toward some misshapen abomination of a piece of furniture.

"Is this . . . a bean bag? How many other people do you think have sat on this thing?" Likotsi glared at the satin-covered lump, but when Fab flopped into it and looked up at her expectantly, she followed her.

The small, beady material inside shifted in a wave as she perched on the rounded edge of it, rolling Fab closer to her.

"I feel like I'm in the ball pit at a children's gymnasium." She settled into the bean bag more firmly, then inhaled deeply. The incense really was quite strong. "I hope you haven't brought me to some kind of opium den. I'm on vacation, but I should still avoid situations where—"

"Likotsi," Fab chided, but then laughed, settling a bit closer. "I'm really going to need to know what kind of life you're living where your first assumptions about places I take you are organ thievery and opium dens. *Chill.*"

Her hand rested on Likotsi's shoulder for a second, the briefest press that made her realize she was sitting stiffly with her hands on her knees.

"All right." She shimmied her shoulders to loosen them and then allowed herself to recline into the bean bag. She wasn't a fan of the texture, but it was comfortable once you relaxed a bit.

Fab lay back beside Likotsi. "It's art. Like, the music sounds different when you're in different parts of the room. The incense is supposed to relax you. And you can just sit and clear your mind. It's like . . . an escape."

"Oh goddess, don't tell me we're locked in here." Likotsi sat up alarmed. "I'm not paying to be locked in a room and forced to solve problems."

Fab rolled her eyes. "Not an escape room. An escape. From the world."

There was something in Fab's tone that grabbed Likotsi's attention—maybe it was the way Fab spoke so evenly, trying to make it seem as if everyone wanted an escape from the world.

"What do you have to escape from?" Likotsi asked gently.

When Fab looked over at her, her eyes were glossy. "You."

Any gentleness that had been in Likotsi was leached out of her by the twist of her heart. Fab was looking at her wide-eyed and teary, as if she wasn't the architect of the misery hut Likotsi had shut herself in for nearly eight months. Was Likotsi supposed to pity her? The hand that rested between her and Fab balled slowly into a fist.

She sucked her teeth, a long, annoyed sound that her grandmother would have been proud of. "You managed that quite well last May. There wasn't very much for you to escape from and you're the one who brought me here."

Fab shook her head but didn't meet Likotsi's eyes. "I've thought about you every day, but I didn't realize how much I'd missed you until I saw you on the train and felt like I couldn't breathe."

"Then why didn't you message me back?" Likotsi asked in a harsh whisper. She tried to sit up and give Fab her stern look, the one she usually saved for overly self-important diplomats, but she sank more deeply into the bean bag. "We could have been talking all this time. I've been here for months."

"Because I kept hoping that one day I'd wake up and I wouldn't think of you." Fab spoke slowly, with a resignation that Likotsi knew in her bones even if she couldn't understand why Fab, breaker of hearts, would be experiencing that emotion. Fab leaned back on the bean bag and closed her eyes. "And because it couldn't lead to anything. Neither of us wanted to do a long-distance relationship, remember? You were supposed to leave and not come back."

"Well, that's what we said on the first date." Likotsi leaned back and stared up at the stream of orange light being projected onto the ceiling. It was actually quite mesmerizing, how it flowed quickly in some places and slower in others. Like rivers. Like blood. Like hope. "By the last date I'd thought . . ."

"I know," Fab said, taking her hand again. She cradled Likotsi's fingers so gently now, not holding them tightly, and Likotsi wondered if that meant she had changed her mind about not letting go.

That was a flight of fancy, not fact.

"Why are you being so mysterious?" She squeezed Fab's hand. "You aren't ill, are you?"

The thought of having found Fab only to lose her left a sick knot of worry in Likotsi's throat. She'd wanted to say goodbye to Fab forever today, on some level. That had been her plan. But there was goodbye and there was *goodbye*.

"I'm not sick." Fab rolled her head to the side and they looked at each other. "It's kind of silly when compared to that. I'm just . . . everything I thought I was gonna do with my life? Got pushed to the side. Because of family. And I don't regret it, because I love my family, but I resent it. Man, do I resent it."

Likotsi understood Fab's reticence now—her story was also someone else's. And Likotsi wasn't Fab's girlfriend, to trust with the heavy secrets of the heart. But this was something. Even if it wasn't what she wanted to know, which was everything, it was clear that Fab hadn't ghosted. Not really. She'd been overwhelmed, jettisoning objects that she couldn't deal with at the time.

It still hurt Likotsi that she'd been in the reject pile, but at least there was a reason—one better than the awful fear Likotsi had let fester in her heart.

She simply didn't care.

Likotsi wiggled her arm, the movement getting Fab's attention. "I might be able to help. I know people. All kinds of people who deal with all kinds of things."

Fab glanced at her, a bittersweet smile on her face.

"Thanks for offering. I don't think you can help with this. And I'm just being a punk. My family has had it much harder than me. I'll get back on track eventually."

They sat in silence, and after a while Likotsi heard light snores coming from beside her. Fab was asleep, face slack and lips slightly parted. Likotsi settled closer to her, wondering what they would do when she awakened, and what would happen if, this time around, she was a part of Fab's *eventually.*

Chapter Six

The Previous Spring

FAB SPENT THE train ride to Midtown trying not to think of what a bad idea a second date with Likotsi was. She'd woken up tangled in her sheets and Likotsi's limbs, her unwrapped hair a mess and her desire still unsatiated. And then Likotsi had pulled on her somehow still unwrinkled suit, kissed Fab hard on the mouth, and asked if they could see each other one more time.

"Aren't you leaving?" Fab had asked.

"Soon. But not yet."

"Then tonight. Definitely tonight." Her day would be spent going to work, then heading to Tati Lise's for a quick supportive dinner, but afterward—she'd catch up on restocking her most popular jewelry designs when this thing with Likotsi was over.

"I have to provide support at a boring party tonight," Likotsi had said. "I should be done around twenty—

eight-thirty. Do you want to come have dinner at the Plaza?"

Fab had squinted sleepily up at Likotsi. "Is that a restaurant?"

"No, the hotel," Likotsi had said, neatly knotting her tie without even looking in a mirror.

Fab had glanced up at Likotsi with a furrowed brow. "The Plaza. Hotel?"

"No, the Plaza Youth Hostel," Likotsi had joked, easily catching the bra Fab grabbed and tossed at her in retaliation.

"I'm in a suite, so you don't—we don't—" Likotsi's face had gone all soft and shy, and she'd crushed the bra cups in her hand, which Fab found somehow endearing given the night they'd spent together. "There's not just going to be me, you, and a bed. We can go out for dinner if you'd like, but the room service is excellent and the view is divine."

Fab had shaken her head. That Likotsi didn't understand how wild it was asking someone to come to a suite at the damn Plaza said a lot. "Me, you, and a bed sounds like a good time. Dinner would be good, too."

She'd risen from her own bed, already half an hour behind her usual morning prework schedule, but with time to spare. Then Likotsi had kissed her goodbye, a kiss that had gone on and on, deeper and hotter and wetter and *lower*, eventually resulting in Fab's first late warning from her boss.

Now, after a day of constantly losing her place in her

spreadsheets because she'd kept thinking back to her date with Likotsi and a night trying to convince her aunt that everything would be all right and that by Friday they'd be having a celebration dinner instead of one shrouded by worry, she found herself at the Plaza Hotel. She was in an elevator with doors made of gold-plated iron bars and staffed with an actual operator, who awkwardly accompanied her on the ride up to the penthouse.

She looked at herself in the reflective surface of the door—shining clean and spotless—and for the first time in a long time felt underdressed. She wore a high-waisted blue and orange flared skirt, a matching orange sleeveless sweetheart top, and black heels. But the elevator was freaking ornate, golden luxury.

The elevator operator, clad in an ill-fitting mauve uniform, glanced at her for the twentieth time during the interminable ride and she finally turned and caught them in the act. "Why are you looking at me like my name is Vivian Ward and you're wondering whether to tell the hotel manager about me?"

The operator's cheeks went pink. "No! I, uh, follow you on InstaPhoto."

"Oh!" Fab lowered her defenses. "Sorry. I'm just a little nervous."

"Well . . ." The elevator operator looked around. "I hear the occupants of this suite always have ladies in and out when they visit Manhattan. Not this week, and I've never heard anything bad, but be careful."

Fab didn't love that information, but she gave the operator her best smile. She knew what a risk it was for someone in service to rat out a rich and important client.

"Good lookin' out." She winked. "I'll post a pic especially for you tomorrow."

The operator's cheeks pinkened even more, and then the elevator door opened.

"Here we are," they said.

Fab considered riding back down, but then she reminded herself that none of this mattered. This was a bonus date, not one she was building a future on. Who cared if Likotsi was a player?

Um, I kind of do, her heart piped up.

"Thanks," she said. "And good night."

"Have a good night, ma'am," the operator said.

The elevator left her directly in front of the suite's clean white door, and she raised her hand to knock when the door opened swiftly, leaving her knuckles inches from the nose of an older white man with gray hair and a stern expression on his face. He was definitely cat daddy material, but Fab wasn't interested.

"I think I have the wrong room?" Fab peeked over his shoulder at the suite that looked like something out of a profile on, well, rich old men who looked like the one who had opened the door.

The man's face softened a bit with reserved amusement. "No. Ms. Adelele is, ah, indisposed. I'm Horace, the suite's butler."

It was then that she noticed his suit was a more tailored version of the same dark gray worn by the elevator operator.

"A butler? For real?" She'd seen the lobby of the hotel before, with its columns and marble and gold, but only because she'd snuck in to take some selfie to post on InstaPhoto when she'd had a particularly good hair and makeup day and wanted to flex. She was by no means poor, but this was next level.

"This is a lot," she said.

"Quite," Horace replied understandingly.

"Thanks, Horace," Likotsi's voice called out from inside, then she stepped around the door. "You can leave for the night."

"Do you need me to draw a bath or take any laundry for dry cleaning?" he asked, bowing slightly. Likotsi's face screwed up in embarrassment, and she playfully nudged his shoulder so that he stood.

"No. Don't forget, I'm not royalty. I'm just a regular woman." She glanced at Fab. "One who is very lucky."

"I concur," Horace said, stepping into the room to let Fab enter before he stepped out. "Usually people are happy to use me to impress their dates, so I thought I'd offer."

"I'm impressive enough on my own, man," Likotsi said with a grin, using both her hands to present herself from head to toe.

Horace rolled his eyes in a way that showed they were friends, then headed to the elevator.

Likotsi closed the door, a sheepish grin on her face as she leaned back against the door. She was dressed in another impressively wrinkle-free white button-up shirt, with dark brown suspenders and tan slacks. Her sleeves were already rolled up. "Hi."

Fab exhaled.

"Hi. Hello. I just need to point out that none of this"—Fab waved her hand around the luxurious suite—"is regular. There was a *butler* at the door. You have service staff."

"I *am* service staff," Likotsi said, raising a finger. "Horace was trying to make me look good because I told him I wanted to impress you. While the boss is away, the staff will play, and all that. There are perks to working for the ridiculously wealthy sometimes."

Fab thought of what the elevator operator had told her.

"I'd say." Fab stared at an antique vase filled with budding roses. Any one object in the room cost at least as much as her parents made in a month, maybe even a year. Displays of wealth were one of those things that became background noise in Manhattan, but somehow she'd been unable to imagine that a room could look like this. And while she certainly appreciated going for an aesthetic, hard, she couldn't imagine why all this stuff was necessary, except to show that you had a lot of money and didn't know what to do with it.

"We can go somewhere else if you want," Likotsi said, seemingly picking up on her discomfort. "I didn't want to, well, okay, yes, I did want to show off. I can't really afford anything worthy of you, but I had this suite to myself and . . ."

Fab felt a tightness in her chest, a slow squeeze as realization set in. Likotsi saw ridiculous wealth like *this* and thought it was what Fab deserved. Fab, who was used to dates with men who sent her invoices for her movie ticket the morning after.

"No. It's just . . . this is real rich people shit. It's a little overwhelming." She looked around. "I'm scared to break something. I could probably get some great Insta-Photo shots in here, though."

"I'd be happy to be your photographer," Likotsi said. "I wouldn't have to do much work."

Likotsi plucked at a suspender arm once, twice, three times, and Fab felt a truth resonate in her along with it: Likotsi was nervous. Now that Fab paid attention, she could see how Likotsi's smile was just a bit strained, and how her movements were just a bit stiff. She was letting her own freaked-out-ness spread to Likotsi, who had done nothing worse than think her worthy of precious items.

"Thanks for inviting me," Fab said softly. "But just so you know, I'm here for you, not the Plaza Hotel, beautiful as it is. I want to hang with you, with or without perks."

Likotsi grinned, that wide, self-assured smile that had drawn Fab to her in the first place.

"Well, my being in Manhattan right now is a perk that I am most grateful for," Likotsi said as she pushed off the door to lead Fab through the living room area.

"What will you do if you ever get a less glamorous job?" Fab asked.

Likotsi stood at a set of French doors and paused to look at Fab curiously. "I've never thought of that. Historically, one doesn't leave this job for another. You retire at age forty, work until you die, or something in between."

Likotsi's flippant tone didn't distract from what she was saying. Finding a new job was nowhere on her radar. Even if this chemistry between them led to more, more would only hit a dead end, eventually.

There is no more. There's just tonight.

Likotsi pulled open the doors and stepped out onto the terrace. Central Park spread out before them below, the shadows of trees swaying in the newly fallen dark and the streetlamps reflecting off the lake. The sound of traffic barely reached them at this height, but the sounds of the night birds above the park did.

"Wow." Fab stepped up the railing around the terrace, absently noting a table with a lit candle and plates covered with silver platters as she passed it. "I've walked through this park so many times, but I've never seen it like this."

From this height you could see the beauty of the park's design, see it for what it truly was—a jewel ringed by the wonder of metal and concrete reaching for the sky.

"There's the merry-go-round," Fab said, pointing. "And that's the zoo, I think."

"I would have had you over for a sunset meal if time had allowed. The sunrise view is the main attraction here though." Likotsi had come to stand beside her and now laid one hand over Fab's.

Fab knew what that hand felt like slipping into the cup of her bra, sliding over her skin, tugging down her panties oh-so-carefully, respecting the fabric.

Desire shivered through her. She wanted that again—the closeness, the heat, the feeling that filled her up as they had kissed and licked and explored each other's bodies—and tonight was maybe the only time she could ever have it. Even if they did meet again, even if they met as many times as they possibly could, *possibly* only extended to a few more days at the most.

She pushed that thought away, focused on the weight of Likotsi's hand on hers.

"Was that the chivalrous version of 'that dress would look even better on my bedroom floor'?" Fab asked, grinning. "I thought you didn't like being presumptuous."

Likotsi lifted one shoulder, her previous stiffness gone. "I'm just providing useful information. It's what I do."

"Well, heaven forbid I stop you from your natural inclination to be helpful."

"Let's go sit down," Likotsi said, moving toward the table. "I'm clearly attracted to you, and that pattern would contrast nicely with the Persian rug in the bedroom, but I already told you that a few days wouldn't be enough. I want to know you."

Likotsi was looking back at her with that almost worshipful intensity again.

"Most people drop all of this smooth talk once they've already gotten you into bed," Fab said.

"Finding a sexual partner is easy," Likotsi replied. "Finding someone that makes you need to know more about them is not."

"When are you leaving again?"

"Soon. Within a few days."

Fab exhaled audibly, then walked toward the table.

"Right. Yeah." She'd hoped that what she already knew would have changed somehow, but this was the grounding reminder that she needed. "That fucking sucks. Because I want to know you, too. And this sounds weird, but I already kinda feel like I do, in a way?"

Fab wouldn't normally just put it all out there, but it wasn't like she had anything to lose—or rather, losing was the only outcome here. There was no reason not to be honest.

"So we both have this sensation? Interesting."

"What sensation?"

"There's a word for it in my language, but . . ." She shook her head, dropping her gaze to the ground before meeting Fab's eyes again. "Tell me about that ring on your finger. You made it?"

Early that morning, Fab had shown Likotsi the corner of her apartment with her materials and hammers and soldering irons, and the projects she was working on to put up on the shop. She nodded.

"Your work really is exquisite. I bet you could sell it anywhere."

"That's the plan," Fab said. "By this time next year, I'll have a small boutique, or a stand at the very least, in addition to my online shop. I think I can do it."

"Of course you can," Likotsi said.

"You say that with such confidence," Fab said, leaning back in her seat.

"Well, you're the woman I've fallen a little bit in love with," Likotsi said easily. "I think you can do anything."

Fab rested her hand on the table to steady herself—that had been a joke the night before, but now . . .

No. She's leaving.

"Right," she said. "What's for dinner?"

Fab let Likotsi pull out her seat for her, and as she lowered herself unsteadily into the cushioned chair she told herself that her vertigo was from being up so high and not because she was a little bit in love, too.

Chapter Seven

Winter

Likotsi remained awake in the strange apartment, tense and worried and debating whether to *accidentally* awaken Fab to demand that she tell her what was going on.

But then she looked at Fab, lips slightly parted and expression content, and decided to let the woman sleep and, while Fab did so, to perhaps give this "chilling" a try.

She listened to Fab's occasional snores and stared at the river of light being projected onto the ceiling. The river changed colors cyclically as it flowed above her, and she began to feel a sense of calm as she absently marked off the colors in her mind. *Red, orange, yellow, blue.*

The atonal hum of the music drowned out her worries about what, exactly, was happening with Fab. The music wasn't so different from the meditational chants of the priestesses back home; Likotsi didn't go to the temple as often as she should, but she had always loved how the songs could help her sit quietly and just *be*.

She lost track of how long she'd been chilling when the flow of light suddenly stopped, pulsing frenetically in place as if fighting against the flow of time itself. She took a deep breath and exhaled. No matter how the day turned out, it was amazing that she was here in this moment—she'd needed this, and somehow Fab had known that.

The river of lights began moving again, reversing its flow, and Likotsi's thoughts did the same, taking her back through the months since she'd lost Fab. Her life hadn't been relentlessly bad, but everything had been dull. Gray. Leeched of vibrancy. Even her most flamboyant suits, her brightest shoes and accessories, had been unable to beat back the drabness that caught up to her when she stopped focusing on her job. Now Fab was with her again, and everything seemed more . . . vivid.

"Hey. Hey!"

Likotsi startled back into consciousness to find Fab snapping a finger next to her ear.

"Wow. You were in the zone." Fab waved a hand in front of Likotsi's face. "I knocked out, but you might have been having an out of body experience."

"No. Last time I had one of those, I was in your bed," Likotsi said, taking hold of Fab's waving hand. Her thumb grazed Fab's palm, and Fab's breath caught. "This was refreshing, but I was very firmly in my body, thanks."

"Right." The word came out soft, breathy, and Fab's gaze was soft with desire.

Likotsi wondered what would happen if she pulled her close, if she sank back into the weird softness of the bean bag and Fab sank with her—if Fab would taste the same if Likotsi licked into her mouth, and if she would feel the same beneath Likotsi's hands.

The door to the apartment opened, and ten or so people who looked like they'd escaped from a yoga studio's Pinterest board walked in.

"Oh, this is *so* zen," one of the women said.

"We should go." Likotsi stood and pulled Fab to her feet, and Fab started for the door, taking the lead naturally.

Likotsi had wanted to see the city in a new light, and as they continued their journey after leaving the DREAM space, she realized that she was. The yellow taxis swarming the streets seemed brighter. The blinking orange hand of a traffic signal grabbed her attention from a block away. Even the people they passed seemed to have come into focus, swaddled in their winter coats and not letting the cold keep them from enjoying their day.

They walked for hours, Likotsi no longer questioning every move and Fab seemingly operating on some inner spontaneity compass. They wandered down streets lined with expensive apartment buildings that had once been tenements, weaved through the imposing columns lining the walkway of a courthouse, explored a memorial to an African burial ground, and made their way down Broadway, instead of up as Likotsi had originally planned to do. They veered left to avoid crowds and ended up at the South Street Seaport, checking out the old ships docked there and, more importantly, window shopping at the mall.

Likotsi's feet were slightly numb from the cold but surprisingly unblistered despite the new shoes as they crossed the tip of the island from east to west through the Financial District, filled with imposing old buildings and statues of the men credited with building America. She had never understood the veneration of these men, who took their own biases and made them into a country's laws, but Americans were quite strange, after all.

"Looks like we're running out of island," she said as they walked down a street with a cobblestone road and restaurants nestled into the ground floors of brick buildings. The barren trees of a park that butted up against New York Harbor was across the street. "I guess—"

"I guess that means we're jumping on the Staten Island ferry and heading out to sea," Fab said, glancing at her. "Was that on your list? It's free."

Likotsi's list was still in her pocket, but she didn't have to look at it because she'd created a new one in her mind. In her heart. This list had one task, and she didn't have to write it down because it was the one thing she had wanted for so long: *be with Fab.*

"Wait, what's that?" Fab was squinting at what appeared to be a large metallic cephalopod filled with flashing lights peeking out from behind the bare branches of tree limbs. "I haven't been here in a long time, that must be new."

"I'll admit that I've been on the Staten Island Ferry before," Likotsi said. "Perhaps we should check out this . . . whatever this is?"

As they drew closer, Likotsi saw people milling about the entrance. Large panes of glass that surrounded the gazebo-like structure beneath the spiral revealed an aquarium with humongous fish swimming round and round their tank. No, not an aquarium, though meant to look like one.

"A carousel!" Fab exclaimed.

Instead of the traditional ponies, this carousel was made of larger than life sea creatures seemingly blown from phosphorescent fiberglass. They moved in an intricate choreography, some spinning in unison, others moving up and down. Likotsi felt somehow overwhelmed by the unexpected beauty they had stumbled upon.

"I wanted to take you to the beach," Fab said quietly as the carousel came to a halt and the occupants of the fish, mostly families with children, hopped off. "That's what I said, that last night together when we were up late imagining what we'd do together if you could stay here for the summer. We'd go to Brighton Beach, and then to the Coney Island Aquarium."

Fab's voice was hard to read, but her eyes weren't, even as they reflected the rippling lights meant to simulate being under water. There was longing in those depths.

"Well, this is the next best thing," Likotsi said, pulling out her wallet to pay their entrance fee. "Besides, it's much too cold at Brighton Beach today, though some people didn't seem to mind this morning. There was a whole group running into the waves. I considered it, but I didn't have anyone to watch my clothes and 'semi-nude train ride into Manhattan' *isn't* on my to-do list."

She slid into the circular opening in what appeared to be a betta fish, the surface of the creature smooth and cool beneath her fingertips as she traced the flowing fins before settling into the single seat. Fab took the fish next to hers, a spiky finned creature that was a bit frightening in its beauty.

The music started and Likotsi let out a yelp as the carrousel began its circular trajectory and her fish began to spin in place, like a tea cup ride.

"I'm glad we haven't eaten yet," she said loudly enough that Fab could hear her over the subdued classical music.

"Why did you go to Brighton Beach today?" Fab asked when her fish spun so that she could briefly meet Likotsi's eye.

"It was on my list," Likotsi called before Fab's fish whirled away from her. The fish she faced now had a small girl inside, and Likotsi returned her smile though she felt slightly sick. She wasn't sure if it was the ride making her dizzy or the tornado of emotions inside of her.

Her fish lined up next to Fab's, neither of them spinning for a moment, and Fab raised a brow.

"What else was on the list?" she asked, just enough curiosity in her voice to shift something in Likotsi.

She'd been waiting for everything to be all right, but they'd been together for hours and she still knew nothing about why Fab had cut contact. She couldn't point her shoes forward until she was able to move from the past, and because Fab was being reticent, she'd have to lead from behind.

She reached into her inner pocket and pulled out the neat white rectangle of paper, leaning to hand it to Fab even though the signage said to keep your hands inside the fish at all times. Fab reached out and grabbed it just before her fish spun away again.

Likotsi looked down at her hands in her lap. She didn't try to catch Fab's eye to see what her reaction was to the list, written in Likotsi's neat semi-cursive.

Forgetting Fabiola Itinerary
  1. *Brighton Beach*
  2. *Chinatown (soup dumplings)*
  3. *Fashion District*
  4. *Morgan Library*
  5. *Roosevelt Island Tram*
  6. *Plaza Hotel bar*
  7. *Lakay Sa Lakay for the egg/hot dog appetizer*

It seemed silly in retrospect, thinking that visiting places they'd been and places they'd imagined going together one day would somehow free her from love's clinging web. But it had been an action, a decision. A step away from her sadness.

Somehow, it had led Fab back to her.

Likotsi took a deep breath and looked up. Fab's expression wasn't exactly sunny, but it wasn't angry either. She gazed at Likotsi as if it was continents that separated them, and not a few meters of space on the platform between them. The music changed, and a violin-heavy piece filled the structure. Likotsi wondered if any of the other passengers felt the music throb in them, somehow both unutterably sad and full of possibility.

Neither Fab nor Likotsi spoke, but their gazes stayed locked on one another for the duration of the carousel's turn. It wasn't uncomfortable, though Likotsi's neck did hurt from craning around fiberglass fins and turning in her seat to keep her eye on the woman who had her heart. She didn't know what would happen when the ride ended, but she'd shown her hand. She had nothing left to give, and hoped Fab would give her the one thing she needed, which wasn't on the list: the truth.

Chapter Eight

The Previous Spring

FAB LOOKED OVER the three dresses she'd laid out for the gala Likotsi had asked her to attend, the waning evening light haloing the buildings across the street and sending rays of stubborn sun through her window. She'd spent her day at work focused on getting the most pressing assignments done so she could leave a bit early.

And maybe, just maybe, could call out sick the next day.

Likotsi would technically be working at the gala, some kind of fundraiser for a pan-African society, but she'd been able to get a ticket for Fab so they could sneak in some dinner and dancing. Fab was excited to learn what exactly it was Likotsi *did*, in addition to seeing her one more time.

One more time.

Each time they met up was supposed to be the last,

but after three overnight dates, hundreds of messages via the dating app, and a few stolen coffee breaks and quick meals, it was starting to feel like maybe, just maybe, they could keep saying "one more time" and this wouldn't have to end.

Fab didn't want it to. She didn't know how tonight would go, but she was hoping she knew how it ended— with "one more time."

Her phone rang, the sound of Tabou Combo's *Aux Antilles* filling the room. It was in that moment that Fab realized that she hadn't checked her family chat all day— on *this* day.

Goose bumps raised the hairs on her arms. She almost considered not answering because she already knew that whatever news awaited her on the other end wasn't good.

"Hi, Maman."

"Are you really so busy you couldn't call last night? Or all day?"

Maman was using *the tone*. The tone that spoke of such utter disappointment, that contained pure wonder at how she could have birthed such an ungrateful child.

Fab's shoulders hunched. "I'm sorry. Work was so busy, and life, I can't—"

"Don't speak to me of can't, while you're busy taking selfies and trying to quit your perfectly good job for some nonsense." Maman's voice was brittle, the ragged edges of each word scraping against the delicate heart-shaped balloon of Fab's happiness. "You know who *can't* right now? Lise. And you won't even help."

The balloon popped.

"I have helped." Fab didn't understand why her mother was mad at her. She was the one who had visited Lise to calm and comfort her over the last two weeks, the one who went every Sunday night for dinner, no matter what.

She reminded herself that for Maman, for Tati Lise, helping was just what you did when family needed you. It didn't matter if you were busy or had plans. Fab was the ungrateful Americanized girl, selfish, who'd forgotten to check in because she'd been fantasizing about a woman she had no future with.

"I don't think you know the meaning of help. Lise told you she was scared, and you told her she was being superstitious. Now they are holding her!"

"What?" Fab had heard, but she didn't want to have understood.

"They are putting her in detention, sending her to the prison in New Jersey like she's a murderer." Maman's voice crumpled on that last word, like a discarded soda can beneath the tire of a yellow cab.

"Is she getting deported?" Fab's voice was unnaturally calm—somewhere in her mind, she was aware that she was in shock. But that awareness was buried beneath memories of Lise's long fingers teaching her to slip beads onto thread, how to match colors perfectly, how to take ugly old costume jewelry from the Good Will Store and turn it into something new and beautiful. "I went over the paperwork with her. Her lawyer did, too. They said this was just a check-in."

"I know all of that. She's still in detention." Maman was quiet for a moment, so quiet Fab thought maybe she'd hung up. Then she heard a deep inhale. "This government says a lot of things, don't they? It's just like back home. They say one thing, and then they take the people you love and maybe you never see them again!"

"Wait. Hold up, okay? I'm going to call her lawyer. I don't think she can get out tonight, but maybe something can be done." Fab was trying to do what needed to be done, to stay calm, but panic was welling up behind the shock. "In the meantime, I'll rent a car tomorrow to take Angela to see Lise. She has debate tonight."

Angela was still at school, where she couldn't check her cell phone. She likely didn't know yet.

Oh, *fuck.*

"She will come home to an empty apartment," Maman said gravely, and Fab's stomach flipped. "No one to make her dinner or breakfast. No one to make sure she's safe. She will need someone in the weeks and months to come. She will need family."

"But Lise's lawyer—"

"Have you watched the news?" her mother cut in, a note of bitterness in a voice that was usually tinged with sweetness—the rind of an orange instead of the pulp.

Fab's hands were shaking, and she wondered if her mother could hear the clacking of her cell phone against the spun metal teardrop earrings she'd made. "Was there something about Lise?"

"No. There was nothing because no one cares about people like Lise. They do not care about people like us except to wish we were gone."

Fab knew the anger in her mother's voice wasn't directed at her. It was frustration. Maman had half-raised Tati Lise herself, and now had to wait helplessly as her sister's fate was decided by a system that had once been a beacon of hope but seemed to grow crueler by the day.

"Maman, I'm sorry."

"I know you are sorry, but you know—" Her mother inhaled sharply, then again, and impotent fear froze every muscle in Fab's body. Maman was crying. Maman had *never* cried before, not where Fab could hear it. Her own eyes went hot with tears.

"You know what I wanted to talk about with you, I think," Maman continued. "Angela is not an adult. She needs someone to take care of her, and if your father and I do that, she will have to move to Florida, away from everything she knows, everything Lise has built for her. Lise worked so hard to get her into that silly, expensive school, and if she comes here she loses that. She loses even the ability to visit her mother in that damn jail. You are the only one who can take care of her right now."

Her mother was explaining this slowly, but not unkindly. She knew what she was asking of her daughter— the same had been asked of her when she was much younger than Fab. While her parents had worked, she'd cared for her siblings. She knew the sacrifice that went with it, but she, like Fab, knew that they had no alternatives that wouldn't hurt a young girl who was already about to have her life turned upside down.

Fab sucked in a breath, and then said what needed to be said. "Don't worry. If Lise isn't released, I can . . . I can be Angela's guardian."

How did this even work? Would she even be allowed to take in her cousin?

God, if she was, what was she supposed to do with a teenager? The longest she'd spent with Angela in a supervisory role as opposed to 'fun older cousin' had been a weekend, when Lise had gone on a trip with the members of her church.

Panic welled up in her. She loved Angela, loved that girl like hell, but she wasn't ready for this.

She had to be.

"I got this, Maman. It'll be okay," she said. Then she took a deep breath and added one of the few creole phrases she could pronounce perfectly. *"Si bondye vle."*

She got off the phone and cried. Then she called Lise's lawyer, who was very nice but clearly overwhelmed, since Lise was one of countless people needing the woman's services.

Then she cried some more.

She carefully applied her makeup, adding extra concealer to hide the puffiness beneath her eyes, and then selected the red cold-shoulder top dress from her bed, pairing it with black stilettoes. She topped it off with a black fascinator with a small veil that shaded her left eye. She supposed it was a good last date outfit—something you'd wear to a celebratory funeral.

She would go sit next to Likotsi at this fancy event for a few precious moments, hold her hand, and take in that beautiful smile. She would make small talk about the people around them, and try not to think of the things they might have done if they'd lived in the same place. She would cry again, and ruin her makeup, because she was losing her aunt, who she loved, and she would lose Likotsi, who'd wanted to fall a little bit in love with Fabiola but whom Fab had fallen for completely.

She dropped down onto her bed and let the tears come again—they hadn't stopped, really, since she'd gotten off the phone with Maman. The tears for Tati Lise. The tears for Angela, who would be crushed when she realized that Lise wasn't coming home tonight, tomorrow—might never come home again because someone had decided her home was an island where everyone she knew was gone. The tears for her own dreams that would be deferred because, when she took in Angela as her ward, she'd have to provide for her in a way that a new business owner couldn't.

And, though it felt selfish, she cried for her own broken heart. She cried for being silly enough to fall fast and hard for someone who'd told her from the start they couldn't stick around. She cried until it hurt at the thought of having to see Likotsi one more time, know-ing she would never see her again.

She couldn't be hurt any more than she already was, wouldn't be able to stand it, and someone had to be waiting for Angela when she got home.

She picked up her phone, sniffling, and navigated to the dating app with shaking hands.

Fabiola C: I have to cancel our date. Sorry. Have a nice life.

Likotsi: Wait. Why? I thought maybe we could talk about . . . where to go from here, I suppose.

Fabiola C: I can't do this. You're leaving, right? It was fun—let's stop before it's not.

Likotsi: I thought you wanted more. Can't we discuss this?

Fabiola C: Sorry. No.

A tear splashed onto the screen, magnifying that *No.* Fab wiped it away, closing the app with the same swipe. She navigated to the settings on her phone and turned off notifications.

She had only placed the phone down for a minute before the urge to check the app struck her, so she held down the home key until the app widgets trembled as much as her hands were, and pressed the X on the dating app.

Delete? All data will be lost.

Fab tapped *Yes*. Then she opened her internet search app and typed in "how to take care of a teenager + foster care + nyc" and waited for the results to load.

Chapter Nine

Winter

THE WALK FROM the ferry terminal was frigid, with the sun almost entirely set and the wind whipping off the water. The grayness of the sky had deepened, from the early dusk and impending precipitation.

Fab had been quiet since they'd left the carousel, and Likotsi didn't try to talk just to fill the silence. She'd made what she wanted known from their first conversation in the train car, and she'd handed over her to-do list. She didn't think she could offer any more of herself than she had; the day had been fun, but she needed more. She deserved more. She deserved an explanation.

Fab stopped and leaned on the railway separating them from the river. The sun was setting now, and in the distance Lady Liberty stood holding her torch. Fab seemed to stare toward the statue, scowling, then pushed off of the railing resolutely.

"It's brick out here," Fab said in a flat voice.

"That means cold," Likotsi said, trying to make her smile.

Fab shoved her hands into her coat pockets, and Likotsi felt the ridiculous pain that had lodged in her heart for all these months give a warning pulse. Fab had spent the day pulling her closer and closer, and now she wasn't even taking her hand. Did this mean that their date was coming to a close?

Likotsi walked beside Fab silently now, shoulders stiff with worry.

This whole impulsive day had started because Likotsi had wanted to be rid of her feelings for Fab. When Fab had appeared on the train, she'd told herself it was the goddess helping her to find the closure she needed to move on. But as the day had progressed, she hadn't wanted closure. She'd wanted—needed—the same thing she had from Fabiola the last time they'd met.

More.

Sometimes it made sense to lead from behind, and other times you had to take the situation to hand.

"Fab. I'm a very patient person—"

"Patient? You set a goal of falling in love with me on the first date," Fab said, the slightest hint of bittersweet amusement in her tone.

"You're right," Likotsi conceded. "I'm not patient at all, when it comes to important things. And I need to know why. Why?"

Likotsi hated how her the last word fell from her

mouth like a clump of wet snow from a branch, landing gracelessly between them. She wasn't patient, but she was prideful. She cleared her throat. "What did I do wrong that you would so thoroughly cut me off? I know that you owe me nothing. I know that you have your boundaries. But what I feel for you . . . what I thought you felt for me. Was I so very mistaken? I thought we could overcome the things that might keep us apart. And you shut me out."

The icy wind hit the tears that watered Likotsi's lash line, the cold trying to freeze them as she'd tried to do with her own heart for the past several months.

"The day I was supposed to meet you at the gala, I found out that my aunt's annual immigration meeting had gone wrong. I'd told her everything would be fine, but she was scheduled for deportation and sent to a holding facility in New Jersey," Fab said. They'd almost reached the Freedom Tower, which loomed an icy blue-gray as it reflected the mood of the sky and of the two former lovers who walked in its shadow.

Likotsi reached out and rested her hand between Fab's shoulder blades, as close as she could get to Fab's heart that was still proper and respectful. "That's . . . it's unfair," she said. It was an unfairness she saw too much of as the advisor to a head of state.

Likotsi was upbeat because it was her personality, but also because if she didn't, the dark underbelly of her job might drown out her light. That, too, was why she'd needed to repudiate her feelings for Fab once and for all.

They'd taken too much of her energy and created too much shadow within her.

"I'm sorry." She pressed her hand into Fab's back a little more as she said the two useless words, because they may have been useless but they were true.

"She'd lived here for twenty years, and her daughter, Angela, was born here, in Brooklyn. We knew something could happen when she went in for the meeting, but it had always been fine. Until it wasn't." Fab took a deep breath, her lungs expanding beneath Likotsi's palm. "My parents live in Florida. It would've been fucked up to make Angela change cities and schools, and give up her friends and everything else she knew, in addition to losing her mom. I'm the only family member here, so I had to become her guardian. I found all of that out as I was getting ready for our date."

"Oh." Likotsi searched her mind for the right words to say, and found none, so said the first thing that leapt onto her tongue. "That must have been rather a big change for you."

Fab chuckled ruefully.

"I love her, even if she gets on my last nerve sometimes. But yes, it was a big change. I don't regret moving to take care of her, but I had to give up on some dreams for a while. And the day it all became real, I didn't handle it very well." Fab stopped and looked at Likotsi. She looked her right in the eyes, not hiding the pain Likotsi had only seen hints of earlier. She couldn't tell herself this was wishful thinking. Fab cared.

Likotsi's own heart began to beat fast, matching the tempo she felt below her palm.

"You were leaving, anyway. And I was already giving up things that were important to me. I didn't want anything else to hurt, and knowing that I would have to say goodbye to you? That hurt."

Likotsi remembered how cold Fab's messages had been. How awful it had been seeing that her own increasingly pathetic replies had never been read. How it had felt as if a late-spring storm had blanketed the verdant field of her relationship with Fab with a deep, heavy snow, blotting it out as if it had never existed.

Fab shook her head. "You have a weird job you can't quit. I was suddenly in charge of a kid that had just had her world turned upside down. I don't even have any siblings! I had to learn how to be a guardian, how to be Angela's rock. I had to make sure she could stay in the fancy private school Tati Lise had worked hard to get her into, and had to look at the tuition for all these colleges she needed to apply to. And even with my parents' help, I couldn't do that on a jewelry maker's salary."

A tear streaked down Fab's cheek.

"Fabiola." Likotsi refused to cry, too. She was furious and happy, confused and comforted, but most of all, she was hopeful. Maybe a single flower had survived that spring storm, a miraculous bulb that could bloom from beneath the ice on a cold winter's afternoon.

"Besides, it was ridiculous." Fab's voice was shaking with emotion. "Who falls in love in, like, three days?

Who gets so fucking caught up in someone they barely know?"

"Me." The word came out harsh and Likotsi cleared her throat again. "It was one day for me, actually. It was 'at first sight' as they say."

Fab made a choking sound, eyes shimmering, and nodded. Likotsi understood that Fab could no longer speak, so she took over.

"After the breakup, I'd hoped that this ridiculous love would leave me as quickly as it had fallen upon me, but it didn't. It clung like a spiderweb, invisible and impossible to extract myself from. And when I saw you stepping through those train doors this morning, my heart cracked even more because I realized the web was unbreakable. That you could walk into my world, at any time, and that love would still be there, clinging to me. That I'd still want to give you everything."

"You can't give me everything, though," Fab said, smiling ruefully. "We can give each other today. That's what I thought when I saw you this morning. I ran into you on the first day I've had to myself in months. And you said that this is the first day you've had to yourself in months. Can't really call that a coincidence, can you?"

"I believe I told you this saying we have in Thesolo: Ingoka makes no mistakes."

"I don't know about all that. But if this isn't a mistake . . ."

Fab leaned in and kissed her, a soft and tentative press of lips that reminded Likotsi that she wasn't the only one with a broken heart. Fab whimpered, the sound one makes when holding their hands before a roaring fire after being lost in the cold.

Likotsi tilted her head and pressed into the kiss, meeting Fab's carefulness with her own deep and powerful longing. She wanted there to be no misunderstandings, in this one thing—Likotsi loved Fabiola, even if it was impractical to do so.

They kissed, buffeted by the cold gusts off the Hudson that seemed intent on knocking them down. The gusts failed; nothing could have pried them apart as they relearned the feel of each other's mouths and tongues.

When they finally pulled apart, Likotsi was no longer cold—it might have been spring again for all she knew. Fab was warm in her arms; her heart was warm in her chest.

All these months, even during their adventures over the course of the day, Likotsi had been able to tell herself that Fab was just amusing herself. That she was just a diversion. But now the facts had been laid bare—they loved each other—and it didn't change a thing.

"Do you really think we only have today?" Likotsi asked, anyway.

Fab took a deep breath. "Do you want more than that? I'm basically a single mom working three jobs. You're working some kind of fancy assassin or something and don't live in the same country."

Likotsi started walking again, their linked arms ensuring that Fab was at her side. The goal of her reconnaissance mission had been achieved: she now knew that Fab had been miserable for seven months and three weeks, too. She'd thought that perhaps this would make her feel better.

It didn't.

They walked on in silence, the silence of mouths and hearts bound by a problem that seemingly had no solution. Waves chopped in the river, high tide lapping at the edges of the walkway and splashing through the wrought iron fence posts.

The strains of music drifted from ahead of them, and laughter. As they made their turn around an area reserved for yachts, Likotsi saw a small brightly lit area, the source of the merriment, and pulled her thoughts from the shadows cast by the immensity of the new problem she faced.

Things seemed rather dire, but they still had today— and tonight. Wallowing would achieve nothing.

"Spontaneity alert," she announced, trying to infuse her voice with cheer. "Ice skating!"

Fab leaned forward to peer around Likotsi. "Oh, I forgot they'd opened a rink here. That's cute!"

"Come dance with me again," Likotsi said. "I can skate much better than I can dance."

"Look, you told me you couldn't dance and I was ready to risk it all after five minutes on the dance floor. You better not pull out anything crazy on this ice rink because this is a family environment, okay?"

Fab smiled, her sadness seeming to lift, and Likotsi

felt her own unhappiness start to fade. Their problem hadn't gone away, but she was literally paid to solve problems and bring order to chaos. She'd figure something out.

"Come on."

They rented skates in their respective sizes and checked their shoes in, both of them sharing a worried look when the attendant shoved their shoes into plastic receptacles without the proper deference.

Fab tied her skates quickly and then knelt before Likotsi, tugging at her skate's laces to make sure they were secure before wrapping them snugly around Likotsi's ankle and tying them into securely knotted bows. Likotsi cupped her cheek and Fab looked up. Winked.

"Can't have you falling and ripping that suit, Dandy Queen," she said.

They clomped their way onto the ice, and Likotsi skated out a bit ahead of Fab. She prepared to push off hard, leaning her weight onto her back leg—and her skate slipped out from under her.

"Ouch!" Her palms stung from catching herself and her knees were cold through the fabric of her pants, but she thought the article of clothing was at least still intact.

She winced and started struggling to stand, only to tumble into an ungainly pile at Fab's feet, which seemed rather fitting. "Oh dear. I believe that I may have overestimated my skating abilities."

Fab pushed her way over to the wall surrounding the

small rink, holding on to it with one hand and reaching out to Likotsi with the other.

"Are you sure this is a good idea?" Fab asked, hauling Likotsi to her feet.

Likotsi slipped and slid a bit, but then threw her other arm around Fab's waist and finally got her footing.

"No. But I've found that sometimes bad ideas are a lot more fulfilling." She looked into Fab's dark brown eyes, refusing to believe that she couldn't have this heat and happiness all the time because of something so small as thousands of miles of ocean and various large land masses.

The cold puffs of air they each exhaled intermingled, and Fab sighed. "Hold on to me."

"You couldn't pry me off with a crowbar," Likotsi said, hugging Fab close as they took short, choppy steps forward. "For many reasons, but partly because I don't think a broken butt fits in with my plans for later."

Fab laughed and kissed Likotsi on her temple.

Little by little, Likotsi's balance came to her, and she and Fab began skating more smoothly, and in sync. Heavy snowflakes eventually began to drift down, and the children around them squealed with delight.

"If you want to know how much I care about you, I'm not pushing you onto the ice to tuck my hair into my hat," Fab said. "I'm risking frizzy acid-snow hair for you."

"That is, perhaps, *the* most romantic thing anyone's ever said to me," Likotsi teased.

"I guess we should get going. Your butt isn't broken—

yet. What are these plans you have later that you need a fracture-free booty for?" Fab asked, her gaze on the ice and her arm around Likotsi's back.

"Making love to you again. If you want."

Likotsi waited. Steeled herself against rejection, but then Fab squeezed her tight.

Fab looked at her and the right corner of her mouth lifted. "You're gonna put it on me, aren't you?"

Heat suffused Likotsi's body. "That is the plan."

Fab started skating toward the exit gate that led off of the ice, pulling Likotsi along with her. "Let's go."

Chapter Ten

Winter

"You really like your fancy hotels, huh?" Fab asked as Likotsi smoothly swiped her plastic key card into the door of the hotel room they were going into after having an adult beverage, presumably to do adult things.

Fab's stomach flipped with excitement, anticipation, and fear—fear because she'd said there was today, and tonight, but just like last time, she wanted more.

"I'm on vacation," Likotsi said crisply as she turned the knob on the door to her room. "Perks, remember?"

The hotel wasn't far from the skating rink, an old bank that had apparently sat boarded up for years and had been recently renovated. From the luxurious atrium bar, where they'd just had hot toddies to warm themselves up, there was an unobstructed view of nine stories of open air ringed by ornate, antique railings, topped by a pyramid-shaped glass skylight, where planes passed overhead. As they lounged on a couch that would have fit right in in the Jane Austen movies Angie was always making her watch, Fab had thought for the first time in a long time, *This place would be great for a photo shoot.*

The room was small, unlike The Plaza suite, but the ceiling was high and one wall of the room was 2/3 windows. There was no butler, and the view outside the window was of another hotel, but she liked the intimacy and the fact that she didn't have to worry about knocking over an expensive vase if she got too freaky.

Fab made a quick visit to the bathroom, giving her teeth a quick brush with the toothbrush Likotsi had asked for at the reception desk and washing her hands thoroughly. Likotsi gave her a sheepish grin as they maneuvered clumsily around one another, Fab stepping into the room and Likotsi taking her place.

Fab strode nervously toward the window, staring out at the office building across the street and the snow blowing through the canyon between them. It was nice to imagine being snowed in at a fancy hotel, but she hoped it all melted before Angie's return the next morning.

She tugged the curtains closed, blocking out the outside world.

"I wish I'd asked for a room with a nicer view." Fab turned and made her way purposefully toward Likotsi, surprised to see worry creasing the corners of Likotsi's eyes. "I know it's no Central Park, but—"

She gently gripped the lapels of Likotsi's coat, respecting the fabric, and pulled until their faces were an inch apart.

"You think I care about anything outside that window, except for voyeurs? The only thing I'm interested in is right here. Me, you, and a bed, remember?"

"Oh. I see." Likotsi's dark brown eyes were warm with desire and with love, even if it was an impulsive love.

If they both felt it, if they'd both been stomped by it, how was it different from love that grew slowly and with careful cultivation? Maybe this love was a beanstalk, sprouting up overnight and reaching for the sky.

"You know, neither of us are conventional people," Fab found herself saying, even though her initial plan had been grab Kotsi, kiss Kotsi, don't ever stop. "Even if I'm dressed like one right now."

"I love you, even in jeans, Fabiola C," Likotsi said with a smile that made Fab's teeth ache, it was so sweet.

"So why would either of us fall in love conventionally?" Fab was undoing the buttons on Likotsi's coat now.

"That's an eminently sensible question," Likotsi said, allowing Fab to pull the coat down her shoulders. "One might say, there was no other way for us to fall in love but immediately. We know our own tastes. We know what best fits our style."

"Exactly," Fab said, dropping a kiss onto Likotsi's mouth, tasting cinnamon, lemon, and rum. Likotsi kissed her back, unzipping Fab's coat as she did.

"And since we fell in love unconventionally, maybe

it's okay if the rest of this is unconventional, too." She tugged off Fab's hat and threw it across the room with a bit more force than was necessary, making Fab laugh. She could take the jeans, but the hat was a bridge too far. "Perhaps, we won't always be in the same place. But my boss is somewhat flexible, now, and he loves a happy ending more than most. And you really must come visit Thesolo. People always ask about my ring and Naledi's necklace."

"You still wear the ring I gave you?" Fab asked, fingers still fumbling with the buttons of Likotsi's shirt. "Wait, what is it you do? You never told me."

"Oh. Yes." Likotsi's hands stopped moving and her expression shifted to something similar to the face her mother's dog made when food was found missing from the counter.

Fab didn't allow herself to worry—or she didn't allow her sudden worry to distract her. Likotsi was a good person.

But maybe her boss isn't.

"I work for a prince." Likotsi's voice was too bright, as if she could mask the fact that what she was saying was completely fucking wild. "I'm Advisor Most High to Prince Thabiso Moshoeshoe of Thesolo."

Fab started to worry, just a bit. This was . . . a little hard to believe. "Advisor. To a prince. How does one get into that?"

"I was recruited." Likotsi reached into her back pocket

and pulled out her wallet, flipping open the brown leather and tugging out a gold card. "Here is my identification."

Fab stared at the golden card, tilting it back and forth to reveal a holographic mountain range that she supposed meant it was real. The picture showed a younger Likotsi with a platinum-dyed Gumby cut that should have looked terrible but fit her face perfectly. There was only one problem. "This isn't in English."

"Oh." Likotsi grabbed for her jacket, yanking it from the floor and fishing out her sleek cell phone. "I'll Google myself. I'd planned to tell you the night of the gala because, well, the prince was the guest of honor but also I didn't feel I needed to be vague any longer. But given my proximity to him, and how that might be used to compromise his safety, it's not something I can disclose to just anyone. I have to trust them."

"You trusted me?" Fab asked.

"Of course. It would be hard not to trust someone you'd fallen in love with."

Fab took the phone and glanced at it. The screen was populated with images of Likotsi standing next to, well, a dude in a crown. The main search page had a link for an online encyclopedia bio—Fab was dating someone with their own encyclopedia entry. Apparently Likotsi was a world-renowned fashion plate who enjoyed poetry, technology, and weaving on a loom.

Fab looked up into the eyes of the woman who she'd pushed away, the woman who had forgiven her for it, and tossed the phone onto the couch without reading further. "Seems legit. Now kiss me. Oh, wait! We were talking about unconventional relationships. Can we have one?"

Likotsi stared, her expression somewhere between joy and confusion.

"Look." Fab paused as she pulled her own sweater over her head. "We've got some things stacked against us. But lots of people have things stacked against them. Nothing has changed from last spring, except instead of running away I'm going to ask if, for the time you have left here, you want to try being together. You only got to one thing on that list of yours, you know. And I'm hoping you'll change the title."

"Something has changed," Likotsi said, pulling her locs into a bun atop her head. "I work for a prince—well, now you know that I do. I told you once I have a particular skill set, and included in that skill set is making queries into citizenship and immigration issues. I could do that, for your aunt."

Fab froze just as she was about to toss her sweater across the hotel room. It didn't leave her fingertips, and instead swung back to softly smack into the bare skin of her side.

"You can?"

"I'm not sure anything will come of it, but I've been at this job for a few years now. I've seen people with power use their privilege for ill gain. If I can use it to help someone, it would behoove me to try." Likotsi reached over and plucked the sweater from Fab's hand, bunching it and holding it against her own stomach. "This has nothing to do with us. With you and I being together. I will look into this even if after tonight you decide to leave."

Fab didn't cry this time, only because her heart was bursting with happiness. Because Likotsi was going to try for her, and for her family, and because her assistance wasn't contingent on getting anything from Fab.

"In fact, maybe we should wait." Likotsi held out the sweater. "I don't want you to think that—"

Fab grabbed the sweater and threw it over her shoulder.

"I've been waiting for months," she said. "And I trust you. That's kind of what happens when you love someone, I've heard."

Likotsi stared at her, and Fab's happiness wavered when she saw the fear in Likotsi's eyes, like the woman was too scared to believe that this was really happening between them.

"I'm the one who broke your trust, even if I had a reason," Fab said. "I'm gonna make sure you don't have to doubt that I'll stay, that you don't have to plan for helping Lise even if I push you away again. I'm not going anywhere, Likotsi Adelele, Advisor Most High to Prince . . . Tha-someone. I'm right here."

"Oh." The word was a soft whisper of relief. "Oh, good. I don't want to be without you again. I don't want to even think of it."

"So we're doing this?" Fab asked, taking a step closer to Likotsi.

Likotsi looked down at the floor, then back up to Fab's face. "My shoes are pointed at you."

Fab tilted her head. "I'm guessing that's a yes."

"Yes," Likotsi said, her voice stronger, her eyes brighter. "Yes. Let's both of us see where this love leads. And when we are afraid, because we will inevitably be afraid again, let's run to each other instead of away."

"I can do that," Fab said. She didn't have to run to Likotsi then, because the space between them was only a step and Likotsi was closing it at the same speed she was.

Fab's hands cupped the back of Likotsi's neck, her fingers brushing over the close-cropped hair there as their mouths met without the hesitation of doubt. Their kiss was hot and desperate, lips crashing together with a desire that had come from months of longing, months of surety that this good thing between them had been lost.

The fingers of one of Likotsi's hands tangled in Fab's bra strap, and the other hand gripped her waist; there was something in the gentle possessiveness of the hold that made tears form in Fab's eyes.

"I'm yours," she said against Likotsi's mouth.

"We're each other's," Likotsi breathed. "We have been since we swiped right. And to think, people say technology is isolating."

Fab laughed.

They tugged off each other's clothes, Likotsi showing no care for her own fine suit, until they were both bare and pressed against one another. Likotsi's skin was soft all over, and both of their bodies were hot to the touch despite a day spent in the cold—Fab imagined they were heated by this love between them to the perfect temperature for bending and reshaping, how she took a simple stick of steel and turned it into wild spirals or finely spun tear drops. She and Likotsi were shaping themselves into the perfect setting for the love they carried in their hearts—a bright, flashy, shining thing that not just anyone could rock.

"Goddess, I've missed the taste of you," Likotsi whispered into Fab's mouth. Her hands slid over Fab's breasts, palms grazing the stiff brown peaks of her nipples, then down over Fab's stomach, and gripping the flare of her wide hips. "And the feel of you and the shape of you."

Likotsi kissed with her eyes open, and with her lips trembling as she fought the smile that pulled her lips back from Fab's.

"I'm scared to blink," she said. "I'm scared I'll wake up from some wonderful dream."

Fab licked into Likotsi's mouth hard, then pressed a kiss on Likotsi's chin, then delivered a gentle, pinching bite to Likotsi's earlobe.

"This is real," she whispered. Likotsi shivered, and Fab couldn't tell if it was from her breath against Likotsi's ear or her thumbs brushing over Likotsi's nipples. "I mean, it better be real or I'm gonna be pissed when I wake up."

They both laughed then, and maneuvered themselves over to the giant king-sized bed that dominated the hotel room. Likotsi tried to push Fab onto her back, but Fab had more leverage and made sure to come out on top.

"I lead, remember?" She ran her hands down Likotsi's body, one cupping a breast, the other continuing downward, palm sliding over smooth skin and wiry hair until her middle and index finger notched over Likotsi's clit.

Fab pressed with those two fingers, circling wide and shallow over the slick nub, watching as Likotsi's eyes squeezed shut and her head pressed back into the pillow. Fab leaned forward to lick at that exposed stretch of neck, to pepper Likotsi's collarbone with kisses, to run her teeth over that décolletage that had teased her from beneath an unbuttoned starched shirt on their first date.

Likotsi moaned, an undignified sound that was so different from her otherwise calm and collected manner. Fab smiled as she licked down the valley between Likotsi's breasts, turning her head to draw one nipple into her mouth while her fingers pinched and teased the other.

She smiled because she'd discovered something that first night together—seeing Likotsi climax with abandon, without the strictures of her tailored suits and ties and waistcoats, was *really fucking hot*.

She deepened the pressure of her fingers between Likotsi's legs, pressing harder and rubbing just slightly faster. She wanted to give Likotsi pleasure, but when Likotsi's hips bucked, when her hands gripped helplessly at Fab's shoulders, Fab's own core tightened with pleasure, and her own desire spiraled up to her head, making her feel dizzy.

"Yes. More, Fab." Her hands gave just the slightest directional push at Fab's shoulders—downward. Likotsi had said that she led from behind, and she did this in all aspects of life.

Fab took her orders, licking down Likotsi's stomach. She repositioned herself on the bed, shuffling over the smooth duvet so that her fingers still massaged Likotsi's clit as her mouth drew closer.

She licked over her own fingers, the tip of her tongue delving between her knuckles to trace along the ridge of Likotsi's nub. She glanced up at Likotsi, who gazed down at her with passion and adoration, her lips pressed together hard. The muscles of Likotsi's abdomen jerked, and Fab flattened her palm over it as she teased the thin strip of dark, exposed flesh poking up from between her index and middle fingers.

Likotsi's fingers dug into the thick duvet, and her hips thrust up insistently—another order that Fab was happy to oblige.

She moved her fingers away, and this time when the flat of her tongue lapped over Likotsi, it firmly covered Likotsi's clit. She settled firmly between Likotsi's thighs now, her greedy mouth licking and sucking.

"Goddess," Likotsi moaned, writhing on the bed, and even though Fab knew she wasn't talking to her, she took it as encouragement. She whirled her tongue hard, then following with soft, gentle laps that she knew left Likotsi eager for more.

She stiffened her fingers, still moist from Likotsi's pleasure and her own tongue, and slicked them into Likotsi's channel, turning her wrist as she thrust in and out, feeling Likotsi's inner muscles clamp around her fingers as they swirled.

Likotsi's fingers threaded into Fab's hair, holding her in place, and when the loud, unrestrained moan broke from Likotsi, when her thighs clamped around Fab's face and her pussy squeezed Fab's fingers, Fab's own body trembled on the precipice of orgasm, just from the touch and taste and scent of this woman she loved who was finally hers again.

"Come, beloved," Likotsi panted. She tugged at Fab's shoulders again, pulling her up until their mouths were level. She kissed Fab, licking into her mouth hard as she notched her thigh against the throbbing need between Fab's legs.

Then there was no leading, from above or below, just the sinuous movement of their hips as the ground against one another. Just their arms wrapped tightly around one another, so tight that they both could barely breathe. Just their mouths fused and their tongues tangling, and their cries echoing down into each other's chests when they broke as one and came together as something strong and new.

They stared at each other in dazed wonder as they drifted down from their bliss. Likotsi's legs were trembling. Fab thought her heart might burst.

"It's only seven," Likotsi said, glancing at the clock on the bedside table. "Do you have to be home any time soon?"

Fab almost censored herself. Almost stopped the words that were on the tip of her tongue. But this was love at second sight, and she wasn't going to be shy about it.

"I am home," she said, running her hand over the arm Likotsi had wrapped around her. "With you. And I can stay here until 10:00 a.m., when I have to pick up Angela from Port Authority and take her to her church, if this snow doesn't cause any delays."

"And after that?" Likotsi asked. There was no fear in her voice, though. No worry.

"I can slip out for date nights every now and then. Angie is at school during the day and she has her friends and activities on the weekend and some weeknights. I'm not going to be a deadbeat foster cousin. But I think we can make something work." Fab saw something shift in Likotsi's eyes. "You can meet her eventually. I think she'll be happy for me, but you know. I'm trying to do this right, and the recommendation is three months."

"One thing you should know about me is that I find following protocol very attractive." Likotsi leaned forward and kissed Fab's forehead. "I'll do things on my end, making calls bright and early Monday morning to see about your aunt, once you've given me more information. I can't promise anything, but I can try, and I know Thabiso will offer any assistance he can."

A prince was going to try to help free her aunt, who was locked away in a tower of sorts. Maybe this *was* a dream.

They snuggled closer, and Fab grinned, lifting just one side of her mouth. "What's good with room service?"

Epilogue

The Following Spring

LIKOTSI HAD DINED at the palaces and mansions of the most powerful people in the world, where even the assistants' table was intimidating, but she hadn't felt nerves like this before. She could use her wit and pedigree to deal with coworkers, as it was, who stepped out of line, but this was different. She was about to dine with Angela, a bloody teenager, and Tati Lise, who was cooking a big Sunday meal for the first time since her recent release from the prison where she'd been held for nearly a year.

Likotsi was about to meet her girlfriend's family.

She was nervous as a goat before a wedding feast.

Her driver left her in front of the large unassuming brick building that looked the same as the ones around it. She double checked the address, even though she'd visited before, when Angela was away on trips with her debate team. This was Fab's last week in this building—she'd be moving into Likotsi's apartment in the royal town house, now that all her security checks had cleared. She'd already met Naledi and Thabiso, who were both thrilled that Likotsi was in love and mercifully no longer obsessed with planning every aspect of their lives.

Likotsi pressed the button to be let into the foyer, and jumped when the loud buzz sounded to let her in. She took the steps two at a time to the third floor, and adjusted her green and yellow bow tie and re-buttoned the jacket of the spring green suit she wore when she reached the landing.

Fab stood in the hallway in front of the apartment, a bright yellow wrap dress that belled down to her knees, and matching yellow heels. Her hair was done up in a bouffant with pin-curled bangs.

Her lips were, of course, bright red.

"Hello, my love," Likotsi said, kissing the back of Fab's right hand. She kissed the back of her ring finger, hoping Fab hadn't noticed, since Likotsi enjoyed nothing more than surprising the woman she loved.

Fab caught Likotsi by the collar as she straightened and kissed her hard on the mouth. "Don't be nervous. They're gonna love you, and I already do."

Likotsi smiled, her fear leaving her, and the door swung open.

An older woman, face worn but not lined, and a girl who was the woman's spitting image, stood there, expressions impartial. Angie was dressed in a t-shirt and skinny jeans combo like most teens Likotsi saw, and Lise wore a blue A-line dress that was a bit too large for her beneath a white apron. It was strange how she could see different aspects of the woman she loved in both of their faces: Lise shared the same sloping cheekbones and her style had clearly inspire Fab's, and Angela's nose was the same.

The scent of delicious food wafted out of the apartment, filling the protracted silence in the hallway.

"She's hot," Angie finally said, giving a thumbs-up to Fab while sporting a faux-serious expression. "Way to go."

Fab playfully swatted at her cousin.

"She also has Fab's lipstick on her mouth," Lise said. She produced a napkin from her apron pocket and handed it over.

Likotsi reached for it, but Lise executed some magic Auntie maneuver and pulled her into a hug instead. It was a tight hug, full of strength and sorrow—and welcome. She released Likotsi and gave her a nod.

"Thank you for everything. *Everything*. I'm so glad to finally meet you," she said. "Welcome to my home."

"Oh, no need for thanks. I didn't—"

Likotsi was cut off by an annoyed sigh.

"If you don't accept her thanks, then she'll just keep insisting and we'll all be standing in the hallway for hours," Angie said, crossing her arms over her chest.

"And then *I* won't get to thank you for bringing my mom back to me. So just understand that when you step into this apartment? You gonna get this gratitude, okay?"

"Okay," Likotsi said with a grin.

Angie spun on her sports-sock clad feet and went into the house. Lise grinned, shook her head, and followed her daughter. Fab started making her way after them, but stopped at the threshold, looked back over her shoulder, and held out her hand. "You coming, baby?"

"Of course." Likotsi took Fab's hand and allowed herself to be led into the home of people who might become her family too someday soon, if the goddess gave Likotsi courage enough to present Fab with the ring she'd purchased weeks ago. "Of course."

Turn the page for a preview of

A PRINCE ON PAPER

on sale April 30, 2019

Chapter One

Welcome to the world of One True Prince, where the prince of your dreams might be just around the corner. Are you ready to find your handsome royal? If so, enter your name here, and then the keys to the kingdom are yours! Remember to choose wisely—the royal life isn't all fun and games, and not every prince is who he seems to be!

NYA JERAMI RETURNED her ridiculously comfortable seat to the upright position, then pushed aside her braids to remove the wireless earplugs from her ears—no amount of relaxing meditation music was going to make her feel better about returning home to Thesolo.

Before leaving to study Early Childhood Development in New York, she'd imagined days spent surrounded by a throng of intrigued peers, and nights being courted by handsome men. She'd had it all planned: after years of being kept like a caged bird by her father, she would arrive in Manhattan, spread her wings, and soar. That was how things happened in the films she had grown up watching, where every timid girl secretly had the heart of a lioness.

But in real life, the jostling crowds and tall buildings made her uneasy, the subway trains gave her motion sickness, and taxis drove in a wild and frightening way. She'd sat silently in class, biting back her thoughts, and her peers had barely known she'd existed. Dating had gone no better, a series of uncomfortable and disheartening encounters with annoying men.

Perhaps her father had been right with his constant reminders she should dream smaller, want less—the simple fact was that, for Nya, New York had simply been too big.

She'd had plenty of exciting adventures—fighting space pirates, taming a vampire king, being sought after by every senpai in her high school—but those had taken place in the virtual dating games she played on her phone. In those worlds, she was fearless, always knew the right thing to say, and if one of her dates annoyed her, she could delete him without much guilt.

Now she peered through the window of the private jet of the royal family, the African landscape heralding that her adventure in New York was truly finished. There were no expansion packs available.

Game over.

"We'll be landing in Thesolo in approximately two hours, Miss Jerami," Mariha, the flight attendant, said as she peeked her head into the cabin for the approximately one thousandth time. "You'll be home soon."

"Thank you," Nya said politely.

Two hours.

Home.

"Are you all right?" Mariha's face was taut with concern, and though Nya should've appreciated it, she hated that expression. People always looked at her like she was a fragile vase perpetually in danger of falling off a shelf. In Thesolo, she was the finance minister's frail, sickly daughter, too weak to know her own mind. That image had stuck with her well past childhood, and despite having single-handedly rejuvenated the Lek Hemane orphanage school, people still patted her on the head and spoke to her like her dance of womanhood hadn't been half a lifetime ago.

They'd taken their cues from her father, who'd spent a lifetime explaining to people that Nya needed his guidance. Unfortunately, his imprisonment hadn't erased the script that he'd written for her. Nya relegated to the role of nonplayer character in the role-playing game of her own life.

Nya has her little job, yes, but she cannot handle too much work. The stress is dangerous for her, and she prefers being at home.

Nya's hands went to her stomach, which was tying itself up in knots of anxiety.

Two hours.

"The flight is a bit bumpy," she said, gazing up at Mariha. "Do you have something soothing for the stomach?"

"We have the goddess blend tea, of course. That has many uses," Mariha said, and then her smile fell as she remembered that Nya's father had used the same tea to poison, corrupting nature and tradition for his own ends. "I'm sorry. I wasn't—forgive me, Ms. Jerami, I wasn't insinuating! I—"

"It's all right," Nya said. Her father had ruined even the pleasure of tea for her. "Ginger ale is good."

"Of course," Mariha replied anxiously. "Wi-Fi service has resumed, by the way." With that, she hurried down the aisle.

Nya snatched up her phone. She opened her friend group chat as anxiety feathered over her neck, scrolling through the last messages from before her flight had taken off.

International Friend Emporium chat

Ledi: If coming back is too overwhelming, just let me know. Obviously, I'm not a fan of your dad, but I'm a fan of YOU. I don't want you to be upset.

Nya: Of course I'm coming to your wedding! Don't be ridiculous. I'll just ignore the people whispering about how I tricked you into being my friend after my father hurt you. Or debating whether I'm a disgraceful daughter who will visit my father in prison or a disgraceful one who won't.

Portia: Those options don't seem fun. Let me know if you need help dealing with the attention. Johan can help, too. Ask him for some pointers.

Nya: I know Johan is your friend, but that guy is weird.

Portia: <thinking emoji> Aren't all of us weird?

Ledi: Thabiso and I found a secret dungeon in the palace (don't ask what I was doing in there), and I will gladly jail anyone who upsets you.

Ledi: Just kidding, I'm not a despot. I *will* call them out and embarrass them, though.

Portia: That's worse than a dungeon, as we all know.

Ledi: Yup. <smiling devil emoji>

Nya: I'll be fine, thank you. Also, please be careful in the dungeon, or at least send us a map so we know where to search if you and Thabiso disappear.

Ledi: I made sure we have cell phone reception in there and since no one comes down here we removed the lock from the door. I'm not trying to live that Cask of Amontillado life.

Portia: Did you look into those therapists I gave you a list of, Nya?

Nya: Gotta go, flight is boarding! <blowing kisses emoji>

Portia: Okay, I can take a hint. <strained smile emoji> Tell Johan that I brought him a present.

Nya's brow furrowed. She'd missed that last message and nothing else had followed it because Ledi and Portia were together and could actually speak to one another.

Nya: What do you mean "tell Johan"?

The message went unread—it was before daybreak in Thesolo.

Her phone emitted a ping and she quickly switched apps, a little burst of relief filling her when the load screen for *One True Prince* appeared. It was a cute, but immersive, dating sim—you played the role of new girl at a boarding school full of princes in which one of them was a spy bent on destroying the system of monarchies forever. It was silly, but intense: you had to be ready to receive messages at any time, even the middle of the night, which had made the game develop a cult following. Like true love, the game worked on its own schedule; you had to keep up or be rich enough to buy your way out of your mistakes.

She'd romanced all of the princes except for two: Basitho, whom the developers had clearly based on her soon-to-be official cousin-in-law, Thabiso, and Hanjo, a bad boy prince based on Thabiso's best friend, Johan. She cringed at the idea of romancing even a fictional version of Thabiso, who besides being her best friend's husband and her in-law was also pretty goofy. As for Hanjo . . .

Johan Maximillian von Braustein was an infamously attractive extrovert, happiest at the center of a party or in front of a camera. He was everything she despised in a man—self-indulgent, spoiled, expecting everything around him to bend to his wishes. Having had to appease her father for most of his life had made her develop a distinct dislike for those traits, though many people seemed to find them worth venerating.

She hated the ease with which Johan moved through the world. She hated that he always seemed so sure of himself. She hated that when Portia had first introduced them, for the briefest moment she'd felt *something* as their gazes met, sparking a wild, ridiculous hope—but then, like most people, he'd quickly looked past her in search of something more interesting.

Hanjo Millianmaxi bon Vaustein was a two-dimensional character that was the closest she would get to the playboy prince of Liechtienbourg paying her any mind. Not that she wanted him to or anything—she was hate-romancing this character. That was it.

Message from: Hanjo

Hello, Nya. I saw that you were having trouble in Advanced Royal History class. Do you need me to tutor you?

She looked through her prepopulated responses.

A. Why would I want help from a carrot head like you?
B. How dare you insinuate I need help!
C. I would love that. I'll bring homemade treats! <3

She didn't want to insult him outright since romance was her goal, so A was out. B was rude, too, but C was much too close to what people would expect her to say in real life. She hit B, then put the phone down where she could keep an eye on it.

Mariha returned with the ginger ale, hovering as Nya sipped.

"Do you need anything else? Toast? Medicine? A heated pad?" Mariha was smiling, but there was mild panic in her eyes. She couldn't risk insulting the princess's cousin right before the ceremony . . . or raising the legendary Jerami ire.

Nya had her own anxiety to deal with, though.

"I believe I'll go lie down actually," she said, standing to escape the attendant's nervous attention.

It was ridiculous for a plane to have a bedroom in the first place, but she would take advantage of it. She hadn't slept during the whole long flight. Her body felt heavy with dread, her back was strained from packing up her apartment, and her heart ached at the weight of all her worries.

"Oh?" Mariha tilted her head and drew it back. "Are you quite sure you want to do that?"

There was censure in her tone, a reminder that in Thesolo everyone thought Nya was in need of their opinion.

"Why wouldn't I be sure?" Nya asked. "I know my own body well enough to understand what it needs."

Mariha opened her mouth, closed it, then raised a hand awkwardly. "Of course. But—"

"I'm going to the bedroom. Do not disturb me until we are ready to land. Please."

Mariha's confused expression relaxed into raised brows and . . . what was that grin about?

"Oh. Ohhhh. Of course." The hovering anxiousness was gone now. "If you need any, ah, anything in particular, check the top drawer in the bedside table."

"Wonderful." Nya turned and strode as confidently as she could toward the bedroom as the plane bounced over air currents, walked in, and closed the door behind her.

The room was completely dark.

Where is the light switch?

She sighed in frustration. She couldn't very well head back out into the cabin and ask the attendant for help after she'd flounced. She pressed the home button on her cell phone, the brief flash of light illuminating the edge of the bed.

She shuffled her way toward it, and sighed in relief as the soft mattress gave way beneath her palms and her knees. It was ridiculously decadent, as would any bed befitting royalty, and she allowed her weary body to sink into the swaddling comfort.

Now that she was alone in the dark, tears stung at her eyes and her chest felt tight. She would be home, Thesolo home, in less than two hours, and despite all the assurances she'd given to friends and family, she was not prepared.

She thought of the way Mariha had been so stiff with her when she'd boarded the plane. How she'd said the name Jerami like it was a hot coal.

It was a venerated surname in the tiny but increasingly powerful African kingdom—Annie and Makalele Jerami, Nya's grandparents, were respected tribal elders, and Naledi Smith nee Ajoua, born of a Jerami, was the country's prodigal princess, whose impending marriage was currently the most anticipated event in Thesolo.

The name was also reviled in some quarters, because of the man that made Nya's hands tremble with nerves.

Alehk Jerami the traitor. Alehk Jerami the disgrace of Thesolo.

Alehk Jerami, Nya's father.

He had committed many crimes against the king-dom of Thesolo, as everyone had discovered two years before—blackmail, treason, fraud—but the worst among these had been the unthinkable act of poisoning his own kin. Annie and Makelele and Naledi—Naledi, whose parents had fled years before to escape Alehk's threats and died in a land far from their ancestors, leaving Naledi orphaned.

Unspeakable.

In the aftermath, people spoke of how Alehk harmed everyone closest to him, as if he himself were poison. There were even rumors that his beloved wife hadn't really died in childbirth, though Nya was fairly cer-tain that rumor wasn't true. But his daughter? No one thought about mousey little Nya when it came to the crimes of Alehk Jerami, except to pity her or wonder if she'd aided him. He'd loved her too much to hurt her, everyone thought, but too much love could hurt, too.

"Would you leave me, too, Nya? After having taken your mother from me? Answer me, child."

"No, Father. I will never leave you."

She sucked in a breath against the panic and pressed her thumbs into the corners of her eyes, as if stopping a leak in a dam. Nya wouldn't cry. She wouldn't, even though she felt more alone than she ever had before, and was certain that being home, which should have made her feel safe, would only make that loneliness apparent.

I wish . . . I wish.

The bed suddenly shifted and Nya was pulled into a strong, solid embrace. Her nose tickled at the smell of lemon and lavender, citrus, and an almost abrasive floral, a comforting scent that was as far from the ubiquitous eng flower of Thesolo—her father's poison of choice—as she could get. The arms that clamped around her were lean and muscular, and the body it pulled her against was just as chiseled. But it was warm—so warm and holding her so gently that she relaxed back against it for a second and sighed at how right it felt before her fear and common sense kicked in.

Wait—

She was alone on the plane. But someone was in the bed beside her. Had her distress been so acute that it had reached Ingoka's ears? Had she conjured this sudden comfort? She knew the folklore of the lesser gods, of those who gave humans what they wanted but always took more than they gave.

No, this is no time for silliness.

She tried to tug herself free from the stranger's arm because, be they god or man, something really fucking weird was going on.

The hold tightened. *"Reste bei mir."*

The words came out in a whisper that tickled Nya's ear and made her belly jolt, even though she couldn't decipher what they meant.

She pushed at one of the arms from below and the hold loosened as the stranger snorted and began to move.

"Hmm. What do we have here?" The voice was deep

and smooth, a European judging from the strangely accented English. So definitely not a lesser god of Thesolo, and most likely a perverted human.

She jumped up off the bed, listing a bit as the plane hit light turbulence, and fumbled with her phone as her hands began to tremble slightly. She was on the plane usually reserved for the royal family of Thesolo. Ledi had made her listen to those true-crime podcasts, so Nya knew that this could be some depraved assassin.

What kind of assassin snuggles people to death? Stranger things had happened, she supposed.

"Who are you and what do you want?" she asked sternly as she tried to access the flashlight app, but her thumb was wet from the tears she'd pressed into submission and the fingerprint reader wouldn't work. She pressed the button to take photos instead, no unlocking required, and the bright bursts of the flash revealed the outline of a man stretched out on the bed.

"What do you want?" she asked again, stepping back toward the door.

"Hmm. Biscuits?" The question was punctuated by the sound of shuffling on the sheets. "Biscuits would be super. I missed the in-flight meal."

Wait. That voice—

The light flicked on then, and she blinked several times, and then kept on blinking even after her eyes had adjusted. Her ears hadn't lied.

It's him.

"It's you." Johan Maximillian von Braustein's thick

auburn hair was tousled and unruly, his cheeks slightly flushed as if he'd been dreaming of something naughty. His dress shirt was unbuttoned at the collar and rolled up to his elbows, revealing the reddish hair dusting his forearms. His wide blue eyes? Those were bright and clear, even if the rest of him was still half-asleep. For a second, she was smacked with the same certainty she'd had when she first met him—that he was appraising her like a man trying to tally how many goats he'd have to trade for the pleasure of making her his, and he was willing to trade them all.

Then he looked away, his features the very picture of boredom. Just her imagination running away with her again, always fooling her into seeing wide vistas when her path was blinkered at best.

He gathered the pillow, which had been tangled up in a sheet, close to him.

"Ledi's cousin. Naya, is it? I thought you were a pillow," he said before yawning hugely, though he at least covered his mouth. Then he glanced at her, as if he'd thoroughly forgotten her presence in the time it had taken him to yawn and was now mildly surprised to find her there. "Well? Do you have biscuits?"

"No." She realized she was still holding her phone out defensively and lowered her arm. His gaze on her intensified, and Nya felt the English being knocked from her head by the impact of his gaze on her. "The bed. I want to be in it."

"I see." His gaze warmed beneath lashes that drooped as if they'd suddenly grown heavy. "Are you here to seduce me, Naya?"

Her vocabulary returned, reloaded by her anger. "Seduce you? No! I didn't even know you were in here!"

He rolled over onto his side, resting his head on the mound of bed toppings he'd gathered, the better to see her. "I know this trick. 'Oh, I'm just a timid little thing who wandered into the lair of the big bad wolf.'" He chuckled and patted the mattress. "Very well, then, Naya. Come to bed and I'll eat you up."

Goddess. He'd gone from ignoring her at every encounter, to not remembering her name, to accusing her of seduction, to offering . . . THAT as easily as the priestesses handing out garlands at the spring festival. She wasn't sure what was more intolerable, his assumption or the amusement in his tone. He was wrong about her intentions, but, like everyone else, thought the mere idea of Nya taking what she wanted was laughable.

Even the most docile Jerami wouldn't tolerate this disrespect. She gripped the phone and pointed it at him. "I am pulling no tricks. And my name is *Nya*. You might remember that before inviting me to lower myself with a man like you."

"My mistake," he said, seemingly resistant to chastising, then scooted over on the bed. "Well, the bed is big enough to fit two, Nya, and I wouldn't mind some company right now."

Nya paused, dropping her hand to her side again. There was *something* in his tone . . . but before she could identify it, he glanced at her from the corner of his eye.

"I didn't ask before, because I was asleep, I suppose, but do you prefer being big spoon or little spoon?" He raised his eyebrows suggestively, underlining the fact that to him this was a joke. But to her . . .

Nya had never been held by a man before Johan had, apparently, mistaken her for a pillow. It had felt good, in that moment before reality had set in. And now this jerk, who had never bothered to learn her name and would likely forget her existence again as soon as the plane landed, thought to make light of the most intimate experience she'd had thus far?

Of course. Self-indulgent, spoiled . . . he doesn't know what it's like to be alone. For him, spooning a random woman on a plane is just another Tuesday.

"You can be big spoon if you want," he offered when she didn't respond, and Nya sucked her teeth. He really was as appalling as the tabloids made him out to be.

"I will be the *only* spoon. Get out." Her voice trembled and she swallowed hard against the lump forming in her throat. She could still feel his arm around her, holding her close. For the first time, she had known what it felt like to be . . . cared for. And it had been this ridiculous man, who cared for no one but himself. This greedy, wanton playboy with his good looks and smooth words, who expected her to bend to his wishes.

Nya was both embarrassed and furious.

Worse, behind her fury, a small, lonely voice in the deepest part of her whispered, *Go to him*. Johan sat there looking at her with his foolish, confident grin, as if he was in cahoots with her traitorous hidden desires.

She gestured toward the door. "Get. Out."

"I'm quite comfortable," he said, settling in. "And let's not forget that I was here first, Mademoiselle I Want to Be in Bed."

This teasing was so much worse than all those times he had ignored her. She'd imagined situations just like this, despite her distaste for him. Situations where he couldn't pretend she didn't exist and was hit with the realization that she existed and she *mattered*—and perhaps even that he wanted no one but her.

"Your dreams are too big, girl."

Now, he was finally looking right at her and all he saw was a woman to be treated like a joke. That was all anyone would ever see.

Her father had been right.

"I said get out!" Nya had never yelled before. It was strange, how the angry words scraped her throat. How did people do this all the time? No matter. She would shout him to the threshold of Ingoka's abyss if necessary. "You rude, inconsiderate, selfish, arrogant—"

Her words caught on an ugly choking sound and tears spilled down her cheeks, a sudden humiliating torrent. She raised her hands to her face.

"Ah, *scheisse*."

She could see the white of his dress shirt and the

gray of his pressed slacks through the spaces between her fingers as he moved from the bed and stood before her, but refused to look up into his face.

"Nya." His voice was gentle now. So, so gentle, wrapping around her like his arms had, which somehow made everything worse.

She shook her head and sniffled against her palm. "I want to be alone." Her voice broke like a youth preparing for her first flower festival, and she squeezed her eyes shut even harder. She had spent so much of her life never breaking, pretending that everything was all right, and of course it would happen now, in front of *him*.

"Here," he said, then there was the feel of silky soft material against the back of her hand. "Take it, along with my apology. I've behaved . . . I won't say it was quite out of character, but I know better and shouldn't have spoken to you in that way. I took out my bad mood on you."

"It's fine. I'm used to that," she said miserably as she snatched the handkerchief he offered. If her father had prepared her for anything it was that her happiness was always to be at the whim of some man.

She wiped at her face, inhaling the scent of lemon and lavender that had wrapped around her so comfortingly.

"Used to it?" Johan huffed. "That doesn't make it right. I was an ass."

She blew her nose, barely listening. She knew that men only apologized when you made them question their own idea of themselves. She would assuage him, so that he could feel like a good guy again and would leave her alone. "It's fine. I accept your apology."

"Don't pardon me so easily." He had one hand on his hip, the other behind his back, as he leaned a bit closer to her. "Or pardon me if you want, I suppose, but at least don't do it because you're used to dealing with asses."

"Sorry," she said automatically. With her father, *sorry* had been a magic word to make unpleasant conversations stop.

"For what?" Johan pressed, and the brazen man had the nerve to sound annoyed with *her*.

Nya didn't respond. She was annoyed herself—and confused. Johan had insulted her, then comforted her, and now was defending her from himself? Men were exhausting, truly.

He made a sound of consternation. "I don't have any more handkerchiefs, but my shirt is quite absorbent if you need a shoulder to cry on. It's made of the finest cotton."

"I have my own shoulders, thank you very much," she said, aware her words didn't quite make sense. "I'm not going to cry all over some disrespectful man."

He tutted. "Come now. You've read the tabloids, I'm sure. Tears are tame in the list of bodily fluids I'm said to share with strangers."

"What?" She didn't want to laugh—she was mad at him, after all, and wanted to be rid of him—but this was all so bizarre that she couldn't suppress her shocked laughter. "Is that oversharing supposed to make me feel better?"

"Does it make you feel worse?" He grinned at her, then brushed aside a lock of hair that had fallen in front of his eyes.

She shook her head. "I guess not."

"*Gutt.*" His gaze flicked to the door and then back to her. "Do you still want me to leave?"

Nya was aware that he was no longer being flippant—that if she wanted him to *stay*, he would do that, too. Her head spun a bit at how quickly Johan could change the flow of the conversation, but then she shook it for a second time. This wasn't a game. He wasn't her one true prince. In the end, he was just another tiresome man who wanted something from her.

"No," she said. "You should go."

"*Comme tu willst,*" he said softly. "The light switch is on the console on the bedside table next to the electrical outlet."

With that he let himself out, taking the bundled top sheet with him. She wouldn't conjecture why, given his whole bodily fluids thing. Instead, she flopped down onto the bed, still somewhat in shock.

Maybe it was for the best she was returning home. She would go back to work at the orphanage school, where the children needed her. She would resume visiting her grandparents, who loved her. She would once again be boring, timid Nya, because that's who she was anywhere she went and she might as well stop trying to be someone she wasn't.

Her phone buzzed in her hand.

NEW MESSAGE FROM HANJO

I like a girl with spirit! I'll be in the library tomorrow afternoon, and we can pretend it's a coincidence when you show up and sit beside me.

"Shut up, Hanjo," she muttered.

She was about to put the phone down when she remembered the flash she'd used to figure out whether Johan was a snuggly stowaway—she had taken photos of him. She shouldn't have felt a gnawing curiosity as she navigated to the camera roll—it was kind of creepy having the photos, even if she hadn't taken them intentionally.

There were eight pictures. Most were dark with blurry patches of light, but one was as clear as if she'd taken it on purpose. She expected his expression to be sly playboy boredom, a wicked grin to match his words in the darkness, but his expression was somber as he looked toward the camera. He looked . . . sad?

No, he looks like a man about to bother you for no reason, because that's what he did, she reminded herself. Then she looked closer.

Was that?

No, it couldn't be.

But it was.

There, poking out from underneath the playboy prince of Liechtienbourg, was the face of a small, ratty, oddly disgruntled-looking teddy bear.

"Oh, goddess," she whispered, not quite sure what to feel. He was a *very* weird man—not because he slept with a teddy bear, but because from everything she knew about him, he was the last man who would. He slept with models, and drove fancy cars, and . . .

Well, it didn't matter. She doubted she'd see him, or his teddy, much after the plane landed, anyway. He was the loud, in the middle of the action type. She was usually safely holding up a wall, looking at those types in admiring scorn. She'd keep his teddy bear secret safe. She would *not* think about how it was rather cute.

She put her phone down and opened the drawer the flight attendant had told her about, in search of a handkerchief. She found a box of thick, aloe-infused tissues—along with condoms, lubricant, and a pair of fuzzy handcuffs.

She remembered the flight attendant's smirk when Nya had insisted on going into the bedroom.

Nya slammed the drawer shut, curled up on the bed, and pulled the pillow over her head. It smelled of eng, but faintly, very faintly, of lemon and lavender.

She sighed.

If Mariha was a gossip, the Nya of the fantasy world would once again be much more interesting than the real one.

Can't wait until April to read another Reluctant Royals story? Well, you're in luck! Another steamy, fun Reluctant Royals novella is coming very soon!

CAN'T ESCAPE LOVE

On sale March 5, 2019!

About the Author

ALYSSA COLE is an award-winning author of historical, contemporary, and sci-fi romance. Her books have received critical acclaim from *The New York Times*, *Library Journal*, BuzzFeed, *Kirkus*, *Booklist*, Jezebel, Vulture, Book Riot, *Entertainment Weekly*, and various other outlets. When she's not working, she can usually be found watching anime with her husband or wrangling their menagerie of animals.

Discover great authors, exclusive offers, and more at hc.com.